Regina: The Darkness Book Two

By D M Singh

D M Singh

For the misfits and nerds. For those out there who don't follow the crowd or feel like you've missed a step and face-planted into your life. This one is for you. Love yourself, embrace your oddities and uniqueness.

You are the real resistance!

Character Cheat sheet

Regina Grace Vasilescu
Hybrid Witch and Vampire.

Emile Vasilescu
Vampire, Regina's father

Evelyn Frieda Vasilescu
Healing Witch, Regina's mother

Martha Anita Shipton
Regina's aunt & powerful, warrior witch

John Shipton
Martha's Husband, warrior wizard

Zachary & Francis Shipton   -
Eldest twins of John and Martha

Violet & Daisy Shipton
Youngest twin daughters of John and Martha

William Shipton
Youngest child of Martha and John

Jane & Henry Johnson

Former spies for Helena turned good (vampires).

Imogen Johnson

Former best friend of Regina – Vampire and daughter of Henry and Jane.

Poppy

Nymph, friend to Regina and resistance member.

Sheeva

Nymph and spy within the council for the resistance

Thomas

Leader of the resistance and changeling wizard

Jay

Hybrid, half elf, half human.

Fem

Jay's mother, elf and resistance member

Gerald

Former pet of Poppy's, now Regina's.

Eli Masters
Chair of the Council of Elders

Lithiana
Representative of the elves on the council of elders

Helena Vanture
Mother of the last hybrid and oldest living vampire

Aurora Trenelle
Helena's assistant and evil lackey (vampire).

To

My Flower

Love you hun, thanks

for everything

JaSyg

Acknowledgements

There are lots of people who have been instrumental in Regina's second instalment coming to fruition.

Always and forever first, my husband Pete, who not only supports me in all I do but edits, beta-reads, checks details and anything else I ask him to. Thank you, thank you honey. I love you x

The amazing JC Clark of The Graphics Shed, your fabulous artwork for my cover blew my mind, you reached into my brain and picked exactly what I wanted. Amazing!

Last but not least my support network of friends that have read, re-read and helped me get Reggie into shape. You're amazing and I love you all. Sherri A Wingler, Heather Lea, Chris Turnbull and Becky Harrison.

The land of others

Long before the time of men or beasts, before anything, magical or not. There was the other place, it had been prepared and it stood waiting.
It would be the best of places, a place all would strive to get to: it was filled with love, harmony and above all, hope.
Men and beasts were born, then came the magic ones, then the blood spillers, then all manner of creatures magical and not. Men, didn't know about the other place and those who did thought of it as heaven, they did not understand what it was, not the way the magic ones did.

The magic ones knew what the place was because magic had created it and so they were connected.
They told others of this place, a place where death could not touch anyone, where all could be free and happy and healthy forever.
One day, one of the magic ones crossed over to this place and took with him a blood spiller, a woman whom he loved fiercely and could not bear to be without.
She agreed that when his time came she would follow him but this was against the ways of the other place.

Though her body had long since died, her spirit had never passed on and so she could not dwell there. After one glorious day together in the other place the magic one and the blood spiller slept. When they awoke they had been parted once more. The blood spiller had been returned to the land of the living and the magic one remained in the land of the others. Both tried everything they could to be reunited but as the magic ones spirit had passed on, he could not become a blood spiller and the blood spiller did not think that she could be killed, though she tried and tried.

Years passed, the magic one grew bitter; he sewed his seeds of discontent and hatred amongst those in the other place. He became a master of deceit and malice.

He preyed on the weaknesses of those who missed their loved ones, telling them lies and half-truths. Soon the place of hope, love and harmony became toxic and poisoned. The magic one wanted everyone to feel the pain he was in, he thought if everyone was as miserable as he, then he would feel better and he did ... for a little while.

Since the beginning of all that is, a passage led the way from the land of the living to the other place. But the hate of the other place seeped into the passage and severed the path, blocking the way through.

The magic one was delighted, all those in the other place were now filled with the same rage and heartache he was, because their loved ones could never come through the passage. Those who died and tried to pass through were trapped in eternal darkness, neither in this place or that; most driven mad with nothing but memories and regret for company.

The day came however, that the blood spiller who had loved the magic one so passionately discovered a way to die and believed that she would at last be with her love. But the damage was done, the bitterness of the magic one had ruined any chance of their reunion. The blood spiller was trapped forever in darkness, driven mad by the love she had lost.

Any who try to enter remain in The Darkness, never to return and so it remains until the two can be reunited.

D M Singh

★Prologue★

How could this be? This moment of happiness becoming a putrid horror-filled one.

Regina looked into the faces of friends old and new and felt her heart break for the pain she had caused them, the pain she would inflict on their families and friends. Thoughts of her old life and home were a million miles away, a lifetime ago. A life she could never recapture or return to, no matter how hard she tried.

Helena had known her for what she was all along, for all her insanity she was right about this. There was no escaping it. She was a monster.

This was it, here at the end of all things, her family lost, her friends too and Jay. It hurt to think that her darkness would most likely kill him. She would never see his smile again, hear his laugh or feel his hand in hers.

The winds screamed, an inhuman sound that chilled Regina through. And as the abyss of dark and despair enveloped her, all she could think was, Helena was right. Then her eyes closed in surrender and with no more fight left in her, she felt the world tear open and she fell.

D M Singh

Chapter 1
In Darkness

Regina's eyes opened. She crouched ready to attack. Her heart responded in kind by slowing so she could hear the danger around, without blood pumping in her ears. She could feel Imogen, Poppy and Aurora in The Darkness. Even with her unusually attuned senses she could not see them, such was the depth of darkness in this place. Well named, she thought to herself as she tried again to adjust her vision and strained to see anything. Silence punctuated only by the drumming of her own heart collapsed in on her. Black pressed at her from every corner, squeezing the air from her lungs, her heart quickened in response.

She felt a hand on her arm and feeling the coolness knew it was Imogen. After Imogen's betrayal it took every ounce of strength not to grab her and give into her own darkness. A part of her shouted for her to, but it was quieted by the part of her that knew she needed Imogen's help, if she was to ever find Jay and get out of this place.

'Is everyone in one piece?' Poppy's voice was like a beacon in the dark, clear and warm and Regina felt instantly easier that there was at least one person on this rescue mission who could be counted on.

'Barely,' Aurora grumped. 'Let's get out of here,' she said in an uncharacteristically quiet voice. It was strangely comforting to know that monsters such as Aurora could be scared too.

'We need to keep moving,' Imogen interjected, still gripping Regina's arm pulling her along. This place sent a chill through her that seemed to permeate her completely, she was not about to argue.

After a few minutes they paused. Aurora made an impatient hissing noise, which was followed by a cry of pain as Imogen pinned her to the ground, all patience gone.

'Okay, we get it, it's creepy here and you don't like it. Tough! NOW SIT DOWN AND SHUT UP UNTIL WE FIGURE OUT OUR NEXT MOVE.' There was a second of scuffling as Aurora contemplated rebellion but then thought better of it.

The earth was scorched, cracking beneath her feet, above indigo hues spotted with swirls of smoke resembling the beginnings of small twisters hung in the air above. Everything about this place screamed run!

A second later they were bathed in light, shimmers of gold and orange that resembled burning embers from a dying hearth, the last sparks igniting and rising up to light the air above. Light did little to assuage the uneasiness they all felt. Regina squinted, all around burnt trees dotted the otherwise deserted landscape.

'How did you do that?' Imogen said as she reached out to touch a glittering spark just in front of her, as she did it jumped and danced away. Regina looked confused.

'It's a simple spell Imogen, no big mystery.' Regina couldn't hide the edge of annoyance that sliced through her voice. Poppy laughed, a tinkling sound that echoed in the gloom.

'Perhaps the reason Imogen is impressed by your 'simple spell', is because it's almost impossible to perform magic here,' she didn't elaborate on where they actually were and so Regina pushed the subject.

'Where exactly are we?' She asked tentatively, dreading that she may already know the answer.

'You should know, I sent you here before for a little visit,' Aurora piped up, a malicious note in her voice. Evidently the light had given her a shot of courage and her usual poisonous mouth had hitched along for the ride. Regina shook her head, she had hoped she was wrong but all evidence seemed to point her towards it.

'Aurora's right,' Poppy said. 'You have been here before, we have entered The Darkness.' Her large eyes drank in Regina's face waiting for her reaction.

'Yes, but what is The Darkness,' Regina continued. She felt like she was playing Russian roulette but already knew which chamber was filled. Her hand instinctively reached into her bag, something stroked her hand and Regina pulled out a chittering Gerald.

'How did you get in here?' She scowled at the little plant, who was stroking Regina's hand with his leaves and purring.

'Oh fantastic, I was just thinking what we needed was a tiny eyeball plant to help protect us all from the nasties in this place,' Aurora drawled sarcastically. Regina growled in response and Gerald made a sound which resembled someone blowing raspberries. Imogen and Poppy giggled.

'Sit there and behave Gerald. I have to check on something,' Regina scolded. His little eye bobbed, as if nodding before disappearing below his foliage and beginning to snore loudly.

Regina reached in and pulled out the book that Thomas had once told her she could have to relieve her boredom because it was nothing more than fiction. A horrible feeling washed over her as she realised her suspicions were correct.

'Aha!' Aurora cried victoriously, springing to her feet and clapping. Her voice filled with sardonic laughter. 'The penny's finally dropped.' Imogen shot a murderous look her way and Aurora flopped back down to the floor, a look of defiance flashing in her blazing eyes.

Regina flicked the book open to the page she had read, what seemed like weeks ago. She scanned the tale, though her recollection of it was perfect, her eyes devoured each word, hoping that they would submit and change to a more pleasing tale, one where she could hope for a happy ending.

'So it is real?' Regina's question felt more like a resigned statement of fact. Poppy nodded. 'Thomas knew?' another statement to which Poppy nodded. Regina knew at once it was true, he would try to protect her from this; she knew that. A part of her waivered as she saw Thomas' face before her for the briefest of seconds. Hard to imagine that so many people had come to mean so much to her, though she had known them for so little time. They had become her family. Another wave of sadness crashed over her, her mother, would she ever see her again? She shook the fear away as a new hope sprung up in its place. 'Let me get this straight, according to this,' she indicated the book, 'this is where all those who have passed on are?' Her voice rose an octave in anticipation, her heart jerked restlessly in her chest. Imogen nodded, though her eyes never left the ground. Regina leapt up, her eyes blazing; cheeks flush eager to be off again. 'My Dad. He's here.' Her voice was a hushed whisper. Again Imogen nodded. Regina's head spun with the possibility, all thoughts of how to get out of here and finding Jay melted away in that moment. Only her father's face filled her mind and her eyes with sudden optimism. Her heart beat a little faster, as if seeing him again could make things better just as he had when he chased the monsters away from under her bed when she was a little girl.

'Where would he be?' Regina paced, biting her lip suddenly aware that she needed to feed and given they were in a place severely lacking in blood, that could be problematic. She snatched the book from Aurora's hands, who had begun flicking idly through the pages with a bored expression and searched through the pages frantically for something, anything that would help her figure this out.

'There's nothing in there about where souls reside.' Imogen said patiently after watching Regina tear through the pages for a few minutes. Regina's eyes flared at Imogen's voice unable to hold back the pain and anger anymore, the beast breaking loose inside her.

'How would you know? And how could I trust you anyway? You do realise that he's dead because of you, you and your parents.' Regina was inches from Imogen's face and her eyes shone the palest white, moments away from giving into her animal side, her breath was ragged as she struggled to hold onto herself.

Aurora watched happily and sniggered gleefully whispering under her breath, 'Fight, fight, fight!' Regina blasted her with a knockout spell which she deflected, but still knocked her to the floor winding her. Imogen slunk back defensively, she knew she had no hope if it came to a fight with Regina and even if she had a chance, she wouldn't be able to bring herself to raise a hand to her friend.

'Do what you have to do, I deserve it,' Imogen said shakily, trying to stand a little prouder.

'Nothing would give me greater pleasure, believe me,' Regina seethed. Her black eyes glinted in the spellbound light around them. 'But it's going to take all of us to get through this place and find Jay. I can wait.' She spat, arms folded across her chest, her face full of unspoken promise. Turning her back on Imogen she spoke to Poppy. 'How do you know so much about this place?' Regina sank down onto the gloomy mist covered ground, her breath fogged out before her as she spoke, lingering like a black mist before dispersing.

'Well I've never been here but I have been to the other place and I met a wizard who had books upon books on The Darkness and the Other Place.' Poppy sat beside a confused looking Regina. 'When an elf dies, it is different from any other living being, because we do not stay dead and so we do not pass through The Darkness.' Regina nodded, she remembered that much from seeing her dead friend flitting around a flower on arriving at the resistance headquarters. 'Before we return and start our new lives, we are permitted to enter the Other Place to see old friends and rest from our work.' Poppy paused giving Regina a moment to process the information.

'So…like a retreat for elves?' Regina asked uncertainly.

'Kind of.' Poppy laughed her tinkling laugh that always warmed Regina from the inside out, like rays of light breaking through dark clouds. 'When I passed on, I visited an old vampire friend of mine, who had passed on many years ago and he introduced me to the wizard I mentioned earlier.'

'I think I understand.' Regina said, chewing her lip and realising that surprisingly, she did. 'Does that mean Jay's in here too? Helena couldn't pass through to the other side could she? It's still blocked right?' Regina's questions spilled out as quickly as they sprouted in her mind, her voice filled with anguish. What if she had dragged them through only to be trapped here, with no way through and no hope of reaching Jay? Had she condemned more people to suffer because of her need to save him? The monster under her control squirmed and jostled to be free, rage and frustration filled every inch of her body till it shook.

'Don't worry, we'll find him before Helena has a chance to find a way through.' Poppy's arm was around her, consoling her and Regina's love for her friend pushed the monster back into its cage.

'Unless she's already crossed over, in which case you can kiss your little sweetheart bye bye.' Aurora cackled cruelly, enjoying the effect it had on Regina. 'Did you really think that Helena just yanked lover-boy through that vortex with no way to get through?' Aurora ran her tongue over her sharpened teeth, looking pleased with herself as the others suddenly realised that Aurora knew more than they had thought and that they had more than likely stepped into a trap. Imogen was first to respond, pinning Aurora to the ground, her teeth at her throat, a snarl rumbling through the air.

'You know where she is.' Poppy accused acid dripped from her normally light and happy voice, the change was unnerving. Her head tilted as she looked menacingly at Aurora.

Aurora grinned maniacally, her lips twitching upwards in glee, her eyes glimmered with unreserved joy at having fooled them.

'Did you think I allowed you to drag me along for the pleasure of your charming company?'

'I was wrong.' Imogen said flatly. 'You should kill her Reggie.' Imogen spat out.

'Don't call me that,' Regina growled. 'No you were right, we need her alive, especially if she knows more than we thought.' Regina grabbed Aurora by the throat her eyes ablaze once more. Aurora's bravado faltered as she flinched from Regina's claw-like grip. 'You're going to tell me everything now, or I am going to tear you apart…piece by piece.'

'I can't, Helena will rip my heart out with her bare hands,' she choked out shuddering from the effort.

'And if you don't tell me what I want to know, I will rip it out and I'll take my time,' Regina snarled. Her hand tightened around Aurora's throat, while she clawed helplessly at Regina's hand.

'Fine,' she gasped, after a few minutes of struggling. Regina's eyes returned to normal and she released the vampire. Her eyes still locked in deadly threat.

'I'll tell you but when we find Helena you must protect me.' Imogen shook her head and Poppy started to protest.

'Deal,' Regina said quickly, ignoring the outraged looks of the others. 'Look she knows Helena's plan, she knows more about this place then we do. We can't just stumble around hoping we find them and besides if she lies to us, we can still kill her.' Imogen reluctantly nodded at the logic, Poppy huffed and turned her back in protest.

'Where is Helena?' Regina demanded, face inches from the now cowering Aurora.

'It's difficult to talk when there's a monster in my face,' Aurora hissed, batting her eyes innocently as Regina growled, pulling away. 'Much better,' she chimed, smoothing her hair down and beaming as if butter wouldn't melt.

'Helena does know one vampire who has been here an inordinate amount of time. She may have mentioned that she would be paying him a visit when she arrived.' Aurora reclined, stretching her legs out, a self-satisfied look in her deceptive eyes.

The clearing they were resting in comprised of burned trees and a hard, cracked mud floor. It had the look of a place that had suffered a horrendous drought, as if the sun itself had scorched everything in its path. A sad joke as no sun ever touched the shadowy skies above.

'What business does Helena have with the vampire?' Poppy asked settling down next to Regina, uneasiness carved into her delicate features.

'He knows how to get back through…' Aurora shrugged.

'So, you want us to believe that Helena's BIG plan was to enter The Darkness, only to return to the mortal world?' Poppy shook her head, her eyes filled with a fury Regina had never seen in her nymph friend.

'You cornered her, she knew she needed a way out, just in case,' Aurora continued, her bluster faltering under three murderous stares.

'Lies!' Imogen shrieked, all patience seemed to have been left in the mortal realm. The Darkness was taking its toll on everyone.

'Don't worry Immy, I'm sure I can find a way of making our new friend talk.' Regina's eyes flashed from black to white, her fangs dangerously close to Aurora's throat. A smile tugged at the corners of Imogen's lips. Hearing Regina use her nickname again was a small victory but she'd take it. Regina caught her smile and scowled, chastising herself for letting her guard down. She could not afford to forget what Imogen had done to her.

'WAIT…WAIT!' Aurora squealed. Regina paused but didn't move.

'It was all a ploy. She never wanted you to join her, she needed you to hate her. She killed your father to ensure you would seek revenge, she knew you would do anything to protect your family. She used your love for them to get you here.' Regina's eyes were her own once more, albeit filled with confusion.

'Explain,' she whispered flatly, an ache in her chest threatened to engulf her as hopelessness filled her. Aurora was right her father was dead because of her. She may not entirely be the monster they had feared, yet so many had died already. She may as well have torn their hearts out herself.

'Helena needed your blood to open the door. A vampire here she seeks, possesses ancient magic, magic she used to practice. She wants to become like you.'

'I don't understand.' Regina shook her head, she was on her feet now pacing, wringing her hands. 'I thought she still had magic?'

'She led everyone to believe she did, but I know the truth. Her magic ran out just a few months ago. She has been taking her magic from witches to keep up the illusion, but stolen powers are not strong enough.' Regina was stunned by the second revelation in as many minutes.

'All this, all those people died, so she could get her magic back?' Regina turned her back, she felt sick. It still didn't make sense, Helena could have taken her blood at any time, why wait? The whites of her eyes flashed, hand poised ready to strike.

'You can't seem to open your mouth without venom and lies spilling out can you? Helena could have stolen my blood at any time.' Regina's breath came in ragged gasps, as she struggled to keep it even, to keep control. Aurora's composure dropped, her eyes filled with dread.

'Ok,' Aurora squeaked, 'she engineered the whole thing.' Regina looked confused. Was she suffering from Déjà vu?

'I think you've outlived your usefulness,' Imogen growled. Picking Aurora up by the throat, she squeezed, smiling as Aurora's eyes grew large with terror.

'WAIT … PLEASE!' Aurora's voice shook, her eyes gleaming with tears. 'Helena needed you and Jay to get back through to the mortal world once she has her power. The blood of two who love each other, that are neither mortal or immortal.' Poppy's face was ashen at these words.

'That is what she wanted all along,' Poppy said quietly, shaking her head. 'She wanted to become as powerful as you and she's planning to use Jay and your blood to do it.'

'Hang on!' Regina countered. 'She said the blood of two who LOVE each other, but Jay and I don't, I mean I like him but he doesn't ...' she trailed off as she met three pairs of knowing eyes.

'Come on even I can see it and that stuff makes me gag,' Aurora blurted out.

'The fact that she was able to open the portal at all means that there's a strong bond between you both,' Poppy said. Regina turned away, her eyes resolutely trained on the blackness before her. She would not let them see her tears or the small smile she allowed herself as she realised how Jay felt about her.

In the distance the dusky sky seemed to deepen and an eerie cry echoed through the air. Regina turned back to the others.

'What was that?' She whispered.

'The Lost,' Poppy said, an edge in her voice.

'I've never read anything about The Lost.' Imogen looked into the shadows as the cries began again.

'We can discuss The Lost later, for now we need to get out of here. It's not safe. Aurora, we need to find that friend of Helena's now!' Poppy's large eyes flickered with fear, something rarely seen in her.

'He lives just beyond the Broken Wood, it's not far. We'll be safe there.' Aurora seemed more helpful, the closer the cries got. With that she jumped to her feet, the others following as the rumbles and screams chased them towards the Broken Wood.

D M Singh

Chapter 2
Home Truths

It had been three days since Thomas had arrived to an empty safe house. Regina's family had arrived just before Regina, Poppy, Imogen and Aurora. Thomas had hoped he could make Regina understand, that she would come to see that entering The Darkness was tantamount to suicide. He shook his head, a faint smile on his lips. He should have known, if it were someone he loved he would have done the same. He hadn't seen it till this moment but they were alike in so many ways.

Looking in the mirror he saw the sadness in his features, his lips turned down in worry, even his eyes seemed bluer as if matching his melancholy. He knew that if anyone could help bring Regina and the others back to them, it was Poppy. She had taken little convincing to join Regina. He took one last look, knowing the real him would have to remain hidden, at least until the Council of Elders knew of the situation and agreed to help. He felt a pang of sorrow at the thought of hiding himself once more. It had been a relief to be around Regina, to have someone see him, really see him. Now that was gone, just like she was. He had never minded it before, but now – now he just longed to be himself.

Regina's aunt Martha had been pacing the living room for hours, chewing her cheek thoughtfully. Poppy had sat with Thomas and explained everything to them. Who they really were, what they really were and who Regina was to them. As Thomas spoke she had found memories flooding back. First they were hazy, but after a quick spell, compliments of Poppy, Martha knew the truth once more.

Thomas felt her grief and guilt, as he had explained that her parents had been slaughtered by the very man she had thought of as an uncle. Eli Masters, his name sent hate, like rivulets of lava through Thomas, jolting his heart awake. It kept him going now, the hate, as well as the need to ensure that Regina's family was safe, he owed her that much. Poppy's departure meant that he was responsible for Evelyn's care and watching over Regina's family, until the others arrived. He didn't like waiting. Watching Evelyn slip away little by little, seeing Martha and her family learn who they were and their discovery that whilst they lived happy oblivious lives, the rest of their family had been scattered, hunted and killed.

'I should have gone with her,' Martha said as soon as Thomas reappeared.

'That,' Thomas said slowly choosing his words carefully. 'Wouldn't have been advisable.'

'That poor girl has been fighting everything and everyone, since the day she found out what she was. She saved us. She has lost so much already. I could have helped her, I *should* have helped her ...'

'Martha. I know that you love her, I know that you want to help her, but believe me when I say that you would not survive. You are mortal, you cannot survive there. Had you followed you would be dead already. Regina has lost enough family, don't you think?' Thomas felt terrible for being so blunt with Martha, but he knew that he had to make sure they stayed here, stayed safe. He had heard them talking about returning home now that the danger had passed. It had taken him two hours to convince them to stay. Helena was gone, that was true but so much of her plan was unknown. He was still unsure how many within their community had aligned with Helena. Who knew what fail-safe plans she had in place? He couldn't risk them leaving.

Martha's husband John had settled himself in a chair next to the patio doors which overlooked the back garden. His balding head nodded and a gentle rumbling sound emanating from that area, indicating he had fallen asleep again. Martha ran her fingers through the small patch of hair perched like an island on his otherwise bald head. Her eyes were far away and as she turned back to face Thomas they glinted with sadness and tears shone there.

'Nothing fazes him,' she said simply. 'I wish I could be so calm about all of this. My sister is somewhere between here and some creepy after world, my niece is off in that otherworld probably fighting for her life, my parents...' She took a shaky breath, wiping her eyes as she did. 'My parents are gone, Emile, oh poor sweet Emile ...' She stared ahead her eyes seemed devoid of anything now, as though she wasn't even really there. 'I'm the only one left. If you don't count my brother. How could he just run away and leave us like this, surely he must have heard what has happened. I can only assume he doesn't care.'

Thomas' heart broke for the woman before him, for her pain, for her sorrow. He knew what it was to be alone. All these years never showing the world the real him, moving place to place, changing his appearance and never connecting with anyone. He knew it was a small price to pay to keep the resistance safe, to bring Helena and Eli to justice. He couldn't even begin to imagine how Martha was holding it together as well as she was. She had lost so much and to her, it was in an instant. She had obviously given up hope that her brother would grow some courage and return to his family.

'What now?' Martha asked breaking Thomas from his thoughts. It was the question she and her family had been voicing incessantly since they had learnt the truth. The children had been amazed thinking about the things they might be able to do when they came of age, the older boys were already getting pretty good at controlling some aspects of their powers. Thomas had already deduced that both boys were healers like their mother. They had been less enthusiastic about their powers when they realised the family members they had unknowingly lost.

'I have been in contact with Sheeva. She has been keeping her eyes and ears open for us at the council. From what she tells me, Eli knows nothing of Helena, or her plans. I think the best course of action is to stick to the original plan. I will infiltrate the Council chambers and talk to Eli, I'll explain what has transpired. I think I have enough evidence to convince him.' He patted the file which lay on the coffee table. Its burgeoning insides straining against the elastic restraints wrapped over and over in an attempt to contain it.

'Then I'll come with you,' Martha said with a decisive nod, but Thomas was already shaking his head in refusal. 'Look, you need to prove Regina's harmless, you need to show she can control herself right?' Thomas nodded reluctantly, running his hand through his thinning hair. 'Well who better to give a character reference than the person whose house she hid in for weeks?' Thomas opened his mouth to protest and Martha snapped her fingers, *'Silentuem,'* she whispered. Thomas clutched his throat straining to speak. Martha laughed, looking at her fingers and wiggling them happily. 'Amazing how it's just come flooding back. Sorry Thomas, but you won't talk me out of this. I can't sit by anymore. I've been out of this fight for too long, this is my family's fight and everyone else has been paying the price for it. All the while I've been obliviously playing the clueless stay-at-home mum.' Martha met Thomas' eyes with a glower of resolve, 'nothing you say will change my mind, so you may as well give up now.' Thomas appeared to be mulling this over when there was a sudden snort from the armchair near the patio doors.

'No use arguing with her mate, she'll get her way in the end.' John yawned loudly from his cushioned fort, 'she always does.' He sighed and then returned to his slumber. Martha arched her brow and looked expectantly at Thomas, who nodded, resigned.

'Loquuntor,' Martha murmured. Thomas gasped and rubbed his throat.

'I guess we should prepare ourselves then. I'll have to disguise you of course, after all, the Council of Elders think you are dead.'

'Sounds like a plan. I need to talk to my children before I go; make them understand why I'm doing this.' Martha stood to leave, pausing to squeeze Thomas' shoulder as she passed. 'Thank you,' she choked out as she dashed from the room. Thomas was torn. Was he doing the right thing? Or had he agreed to walk the poor woman to her death. Thomas tried hard not to think about it, as he grabbed the file and took the stairs two at a time to his room.

Chapter 3
The Broken Wood

Regina's eyes had been opened since discovering who she really was, seeing the world she belonged to was both magical and terrifying. She thought she had seen it all. As she stepped through the Broken Wood, she knew she had been mistaken. She had NOT seen it all.

The light she had conjured bobbed ahead of them; Aurora leading the way. Poppy and Imogen trailed her closely, ready for her expected betrayal. The burnt, withering stumps of dead tree, stretched, grasping at them in the dark as they pushed on. The cries of The Lost closing in from every direction. Regina shuddered. A hopelessness descended upon her, settling in her chest and making it hard to think straight. Her monster seemed restless, it appeared that this place appealed greatly to it. It took everything in her not to give in. Poppy cast a concerned look toward Regina, as she hurried through the treacherous woodland. Regina threw her a placating smile. Poppy returned the smile but still seemed perturbed.

Ahead, the mist had begun to lift, just enough to see the hoards that filled the path ahead. Regina blanched as she observed zombie-like creatures floating aimlessly along, no real sense of direction. They seemed creepy but harmless enough, Regina thought as one brushed against her. Then came the pain, so intense she fell to her knees, a feral cry ripping from her lungs. Poppy grabbed her, pulling her along.

'Keep moving,' Poppy whispered, moving faster now. The Lost's closed, peaceful eyes were now open, following them intently.

'What did that thing do to me?' Regina hissed in pain.

'We need to get somewhere safe … NOW,' Poppy's eyes widened. Regina followed her eyes and gasped as The Lost multiplied right before her eyes, growing in size as they did. If they didn't get out of the Broken Wood soon they would not be able to move without touching one of The Lost. Given the pain she had encountered from just one, she could not fathom the pain a whole army could inflict.

'THIS WAY,' Aurora called and darted beneath a moving tree with tentacle-like branches, which was trying its level best to knock them back down the path and into the hands of The Lost. At the sound of Aurora's voice, a swarm of The Lost turned and began to move with a swiftness Regina hadn't thought they possessed. They would never make it!

'Zalca,' Regina screamed towards the skies. For a moment she thought Poppy was right, her magic would not work, but then the sky rumbled. The Lost stood transfixed by this new louder sound, gazing skywards expectantly. Poppy followed their gaze but Regina pulled her along now ducking below the moving branches.

'MOVE,' she screamed. They rolled through just in time, the ground shook. The sky was alive with lightening, flashing violently and cracking the ground they had stood on just a second earlier.

'Come on,' Aurora beckoned already moving. 'That firework show won't keep them distracted for long.' It seemed as though flight was impossible here other than for Poppy, who seemed to be able to do so in her diminutive form. This part of the woods had no trail or path, the sky was entirely blacked out by the tangles of branches, which moved and grabbed at them as they ran. The cries of The Lost were silent for a while, but then they came again, weak at first but stronger now.

'In here,' Aurora said stopping suddenly. She had ripped a tree stump, roots and all from the ground. The three friends exchanged a confused look. 'Are you coming or not?' Aurora snapped. 'Fine. Stay up here, have fun playing with The Lost.' And with that she jumped. Imogen shrugged and followed her, then Poppy. Regina clicked her fingers and her light orb flickered out and she stood alone in the dark. She could feel The Darkness infecting her and wondered if it was affecting the others too. She shook the thought from her head and jumped.

Regina felt like a character from Alice in Wonderland, as though she had fallen down the rabbit hole and it just kept getting stranger. They landed and found themselves in a tunnel, which splintered in countless directions.

'What is this place?' Imogen wondered, as Regina conjured the bobbing light again.

'Where those who are not yet Lost dwell,' Poppy said. 'They hide from them down here, those who live above ground do not retain their sanity for long.'

'Where to now?' Regina asked Aurora.

'We follow this tunnel for a little way. It's not far,' she said quickly, her eyes anxiously darted in the greying light watching for The Lost.

They continued along the tunnel for about three miles before Aurora turned left, right and then left again. Facing a large red door. Aurora tentatively knocked, trepidation in her eyes. A voice boomed through the bloodied wood, before she had a chance to worry about it too much.

'Go away!' A man commanded from the other side.

'Dragmir. It's Aurora,' she said nervously. Bolts slid and creaked as the door inched open slowly. A cautious eye appearing at the crack.

'Are you alone?' He demanded.

'No,' Aurora began, Dragmir grunted and made to close the door but Aurora pleaded. 'Please let us in. We need to find our way to Davina, if not we'll be stuck here forever.' He paused and for a moment Regina thought he would slam the door in their faces and all would be lost.

'Quickly then,' he grumbled, opening the door wide enough to admit them before slamming it and pushing the bolts back in place. Dragmir's 'home' was one room which comprised a bed shoved up against the wall, a rickety looking chair, a suspect looking couch and a small table upon which lay a well-thumbed book, which had obviously been read over and over. Regina wondered if it was a favourite of his, then realised that it was probably the only one he had, after all there was no Amazon or Waterstones to pop to when he fancied a new book. She wondered how long he had been alone, here in this depressingly little room; no windows, no air, no day or night. An endless twilight, punctuated only with the cries of The Lost. All of a sudden Regina felt caged and desperate to get out of this place that threatened to pull her under and drown her in its darkness.

'So, you're looking for Davina?' He directed his

question to Poppy, who nodded, regarding their host suspiciously.

'Aurora tells us that she knows how to cross over,' Poppy said, careful not to tell this stranger too much about who they were and what they were here to do.

'It has been rumoured that she can. Though I seriously doubt it. If she can, why is she still here?' He said logically. Regina's eyes swung to Aurora who was looking nervous again.

'Good point Dragmir,' Regina growled as her monster rumbled in her chest. Her eyes flashed at Aurora before she could control them. Dragmir stumbled backwards, his eyes filled with fear.

'You're a … you're …' He floundered.

'Yes, yes, she's the big bad monster,' Aurora laughed, stopping abruptly when Regina's eyes met hers again.

'Dragmir … why does that name sound so familiar?' Imogen mused aloud, biting her lip.

'It was a very popular name where I came from in the 1500's, very much like your Steve's or Dave's of today.' He grinned. Imogen eyed him dubiously.

'How do you two know each other exactly?' She nodded towards Aurora who'd made herself comfortable on the chair in the corner.

'We don't exactly know each other. I know Helena and she mentioned a friend of hers might have need of my help,' he shrugged.

'You've seen her recently? Was she alone? Did she have an elf with her? Was he okay?' Regina blurted, her eye's wild with emotion.

'Yes, no, yes and he was a little shaken and not happy to be here but he seemed largely unharmed,' Dragmir rattled off. Regina breathed a sigh of relief. 'Look I have no idea what Helena has going on, or how you're involved in it all. I owe her and so I promised I would help her friend, that's all I know. I can hide you until morning, then we travel to Endless Valley to find Davina. That's as much as I can do.' He touched Regina briefly on the shoulder, a gesture of comfort which took her by surprise. Most people were too scared to be in the same room as her, never mind offer her shelter, help and comfort. She rewarded him with a tired smile and for a second she saw a glimmer of pain in his eyes that was gone as quickly as it appeared.

'Why don't you rest a while?' He gestured towards his bed. She shook her head.

'Go ahead,' Poppy said. 'You look about ready to drop.' Regina thought about arguing, but exhaustion washed over her and she was eager to close her eyes and hide from her monster for a little while. Pulling Gerald from his canvas hide-away, she placed him gently on the pillow beside her as she drifted off to his rhythmic cooing.

Chapter 4

Preparing for the worst

Sheeva walked slowly through the halls of the council chambers. Eli had ordered a search for Helena the morning after her flat on the bank of the Thames had gone up in smoke. He had paced the main council chamber, literally pulling his hair whilst barking orders at petrified witches and wizards. Sheeva had sounded appropriately concerned and promised to enlist the elf and nymph community in the search.

Today, Eli seemed more volatile than usual. Sheeva had long suspected that he had a soft spot for Helena. She also knew that was most likely part of Helena's plan to control the situation. She had noticed how Helena would casually touch Eli's arm whilst conversing, how she laughed a little louder and longer whenever he told one of his stories. Eli was an arrogant man but Sheeva had never considered him gullible. She had to admit, Helena had played her hand perfectly.

Eli and the Council of Elders had jumped to the conclusion that Regina had killed both Helena and Aurora. Sheeva would be returning to the safe house today but felt she needed to try to reason with Eli one more time. She had communicated with Thomas through the note book she had spelled when she first joined the resistance. He had been less than pleased with her idea to talk to Eli, but she knew she had to try and find out more.

She took a deep breath and raised her fist to knock, but was called in before her knuckles touched the ash door.

'Has she been found?' Eli bound across his office which the agility of man half his age. His eyes pleaded, making Sheeva feel an inkling of pity for the obviously deluded fellow. She shook her head. 'Well then,' he spat out, impatient once more, all softness gone from his voice. 'What is it you want?' Eli huffed back across the room, he reclaimed his seat, sifting through papers and glimmering magical maps. Little dots of light moved across grids, the squares glinted amber then green, indicting a search of the area was complete and Helena was still missing. Eli sighed as two or three turned green before his eyes. He barely looked up as Sheeva crossed towards the black desk he had clearly not left since Helena's disappearance.

Before Eli had taken his place at the head of Council, she had visited his predecessor, Ermarute Gererad. She had been a lovely, warm woman, beloved by all she met. A nymph who was respected by all the magical community. For over two hundred years not a single incident of bloodshed had occurred, then Eli had taken over. Sheeva never quite believed the story of Ermarute's death. It was extremely hard to kill a nymph, after all they had already died as elves. The office had been filled with laughter and hope when Ermarute held the seat Eli now occupied. Eli was openly disappointed when his old friend had been nominated to replace Ermarute, after all he was Ermarute's number two. He was more than happy to take his friends place when he refused and more than a little eager to prove himself. So eager, he sold out his old friends and cost them their lives. Since then, the Council of Elders had reeked of corruption. Sheeva knew all too well the number of people who had lost their lives to Eli's quest. She suspected he felt the need to prove that he was right about Regina, that he had killed so many for *good* reason. The Death Squads roamed from country to country unchecked, people went missing and no one dare ask questions.

The Death Squads were originally a small group of protectors, who cleaned up the occasional magical disaster. They protected humans and the magical community from one another. After Eli had taken power, he decided a more aggressive approach was needed and fired the original members of the then Magical Peacekeeping Patrol or MPP. They were replaced with mostly werewolves, vampires and a smattering of witches and wizards. Werewolves were not known for their diplomacy and so it shook the community to the core when so many chose to join. Eli assured them how necessary it was, *after all we have a monster in our midst*, he had claimed with great fervour, when addressing the Council. *A monster who would kill our families, expose our kind to the humans and if given a chance destroy every last one of us*. Those who had wanted him out of power, after the murder of Regina's grandparents, suddenly decided while it was tragic, it was a necessary sacrifice.

Eli watched the search grid light-up, roaring down the phone he had pressed to his ear. Sheeva fidgeted in her seat, her eyes drawn to the sky outside. Things had changed since Regina had fallen into Darkness, Sheeva felt it. As a nymph she was intrinsically connected to nature, and nature was not well of late. Darkened skies seemed reluctant to leave; flowers, trees, plants, they all seemed … off. Sheeva didn't know what it was and how it was connected but she felt it, they all did. Thick fog rolled through the chill air outside, grazing the window of the office, leaving an icy trail as it did; she shivered.

'Still no word,' Eli sighed, throwing the phone on the desk, his head in his hands.

'I'm sure that Helena is just fine,' Sheeva said tentatively as Eli emerged from behind his hands.

'What makes you think that?' Eli looked at Sheeva like she had lost her mind.

'Helena is very strong. She survived Sophia, I find it hard to believe that she could not survive this … child.' She was convincing enough, as she knew Helena to be alive and well. 'Eli, can I speak frankly?' Her big black eyes flickered to his, holding him there and willing him to hear her out.

'Of course,' Eli said curtly.

'Are you entirely convinced that the girl has harmed Helena?' Eli opened his mouth to speak but she pushed on. 'I know that she is dangerous but there does not appear to be any connection. In fact there have been no incidents of violence or death surrounding the girl at all since she has come of age.'

'That may be Sheeva but that fact remains that a member of the council and her assistant are missing. At the same time as that abomination is running free. I don't think it's a coincidence.'

'But you have to agree that things appear different this time. If the girl had given in to her hunger or rage, there would be a trail in her wake, we both know this Eli. What do you think that means?' Sheeva looked so genuinely puzzled that Eli pondered this a moment.

'You are right, it does seem as though this one has more control than Sophia did but we can't assume anything Sheeva. If I knew for certain that this … Regina wasn't dangerous, then of course that would change things. However with Helena missing and Regina no-where to be found, it does seem as though she is to blame. Now if you'll excuse me my teams will be calling their reports in any minute.' Eli stood checking his watch. Sheeva sighed in relief as she left the room. She hurried to her office where she pulled out the notebook and penned a quick note to Thomas.

I am safe. Eli not suspicious, proceed as planned.

With that, Sheeva, took one last look at the office she had occupied for a hundred years. After tomorrow they would know she was resistance, if things went well she hoped she would be back, if not she would see these halls and walls again as they dragged her before the council on charges of treason. She sighed and closed the door unsure of what tomorrow would bring and eager for all of this to be over.

D M Singh

Chapter 5
The Endless Valley

Regina had slept longer than she would have liked and woke to find Dragmir ready to leave as soon as her eyes had opened; eager to be rid of them no doubt. He handed her, Imogen and Aurora a bag of blood each. Regina resisted the urge to drain the whole bag and forced herself to take a few pulls before shoving it into her pocket. She had briefly wondered where he had managed to acquire blood in this place but she had a feeling she would not like the answer and so kept her questions to herself. He was helping them and that was enough. She scooped up a babbling Gerald, who made a rather rude raspberry noise and lowered him carefully back into her bag.

As it turned out, mornings in The Darkness were almost identical to the nights. The only difference being The Lost were nowhere to be seen. Making their way through the twisting halls and tunnels, Dragmir had explained that The Lost fed at night and slept through the day in the caves near Lost Souls Mountain. Regina could not help but think that whoever had named this place, had jinxed it big time, The Darkness, Broken Woods, Endless Valley, Lost Souls Mountain; they didn't exactly scream cheerful.

Time moved slowly here or so it seemed, perhaps it was just Regina's impatience which made her believe so. It took hours to reach the surface. When they emerged, it was clear they were not in the Broken Woods and she realised that they had completed the majority of their journey below the earth.

The path ahead was stripped of all life, no trees, plants, not even a tuft of grass. Darkness and nothingness stretched out before them and behind them, on either side two mountains climbed to the shadowy sky above.

'Please tell me that one of those mountains is not the mountain of Lost Souls?' Aurora whispered.

'Don't worry, that mountain is just home to a few bats, nothing too scary,' Dragmir soothed, indicating the mountain to the right. 'This one however is indeed the Mountain of Lost Souls and the caves of The Lost are not far from it, so I would advise we move quickly and quietly.' Aurora swallowed hard and picked up the pace. Regina grinned and was sure she saw a sliver of satisfaction flicker across Dragmir's face at Aurora's look of panic.

'How much longer?' Regina asked, after they had walked further and stopped to rest. It seemed this place was draining them all. None of them seemed able to fly and they seemed to tire easily, as if they were mortal once more.

'Not far, we'll make it before evening, fret not,' he paused. 'There is something you need to know about Davina before we arrive.' The others turned to listen. 'She was cursed in this place, she's … a vampire for the most part but … well she has been in this Darkness so long, another side of her takes control from time to time.'

'What, so she's like a super *PMS-ing* vampire?' Aurora quipped, snorting at her own joke.

'Not exactly,' Dragmir scratched at his beard, as though searching for the right words. 'She is mostly herself but when her *darkness* takes over, she becomes a bit of a beast.'

'I think I can handle a bit of a beast,' Regina scoffed, rolling her eyes. Imogen eyed him suspiciously.

'Well I've warned you, if we hurry we'll make it to her home before The Lost awaken.' He looked at the murky sky above and Regina wondered for a moment how he knew it was day or night, what signs was he reading in the sky?

Davina's home was surprisingly homely and pleasant. It was nestled at the foot of The Mountain of Lost Souls. Regina could hear the bats from nearby caves causing her to shiver; she had never liked them. It seemed ridiculous that she was scared of such little mammals, with all she had seen.

A crooked tree with a thick pale trunk stood alone, the bottom of the trunk greyed and flecks of bark curled and peeled, leaving patches of white that jumped out in the never-ending dark. A single large window was embedded within the tree, an oil lamp could be seen burning on the table within. Regina's heart leapt with hope. They'd made it! Maybe they could find Jay and get out.

'Erm, where's the door?' Aurora asked circling the tree carefully.

'She knows we are here. We must wait to be invited,' Dragmir said simply.   Imogen glared at him. 'What? You think because we're in The Darkness we've forgotten correct social etiquette?' He raised his brow in disbelief. Regina smirked. There was something about him she liked. In some small way he reminded her of her father and at that thought her stomach clenched in grief, awakening her monster.

'Enter.' A voice swirled through the air, echoing in their ears. Before any of them had a chance to ask how, a large door appeared.

'I thought it was nearly impossible to do magic here?' Regina questioned Poppy again.' It seems as though I'm not the only one.'

Dragmir led the way. Davina's house, or tree was bathed in light and was a welcome relief after such darkness. It bolstered Regina's hope. The room incredibly was rectangular and appeared to be much larger and grander than it appeared from the outside. Davina was definitely very gifted, which confused Regina. She was a vampire she shouldn't have any magic.

Aurora had wasted no time in making herself at home and had found a comfy chair by the large driftwood fireplace, warming her feet and sucking down the last dregs of her blood. It astounded Regina that in such a barren, charred world, everything could feel so frozen in despair. Yet here in Davina's home, the dark receded almost as if it knew better than to venture here. The others stood, taking in their host's home. A black iron chandelier hung from the ceiling, it remained unlit. Instead oil lamps covered every surface. It made Regina think of a grand hotel lobby, with art deco couches, bookshelves and low side tables. A door next to the fireplace creaked open and Davina swept in. Regina gasped, though she knew vampires were beautiful by nature, all part of getting humans to trust them, to desire to be near them, Davina was the most beautiful vampire she had ever encountered. Her porcelain heart shaped face was complimented by her deep almost blood red curls. Her eyes were the brightest emerald green she had ever seen and were framed by dark black lashes. Black traced her eyes below and above, causing her eyes to appear even brighter and intimidating. An ebony velvet corset cinched her waist and her heavy skirt swirled as she stalked across the room towards Regina, her eyes filled with curiosity. She stopped short of Regina, her face inches from hers and inhaled deeply. It should have been a ridiculous thing to do but it was not. Regina swallowed hard. She was not afraid of her she realised, just curious. This was new. Even her friends knew to fear her.

'Well, well, what have you brought me this time Dragmir darling?' She drawled, her eyes never leaving Regina's. Regina growled, sick of being the main attraction of a freak show.

'Oh Kitty has bite,' she giggled.

'You have no idea,' Imogen warned.

'Interesting, I'll show you mine if you show me yours.' Davina looked positively delighted to be in the company of a monster. Regina looked at Dragmir, who simply shook his head.

'Must you show off Davina?' He chastised.

'I presume you want my help in some way.' Davina scanned the faces of the vampires and nymph, now assembled in her living room. 'Money is useless here. So if you want my help, my fee is to see the beast in all her glory.' She crossed the room and poured herself a glass of wine swirling the contents, her eyes on Regina, as if she were a grand prize.

'No, Regina,' Poppy piped up. 'That side of you must be kept in check, if you give in to your monster too much in this place, you may never come back.' Davina simply looked amused.

'We need her help, if this is the price I'll gladly pay it, if it means we can get home, if it means we could save Jay,' Regina reasoned. 'Fine, I'll show you.' She glanced around. 'Outside, if I lose control in here I can't guarantee anyone's safety.'

'Perfect,' Davina purred, draining her glass, looking like a child on Christmas morning.

The air outside had grown thicker and Regina instinctively knew it was nearly night, even though the blackened skies never gave way to lighter ones. She guessed the thick atmosphere had something to do with The Lost and the despair they brought with them.

It was easier to change here, her monster was eager to be free, to kill, to feed. Staring into Davina's eyes, she felt the change come, white hot and familiar, like a warm blanket. Her eyes flickered from black to white, her lips curled up into a scream to rival any Banshee. For a second she thought there was something important she had to do, someone to find but then it was gone and all she felt was the hunger, the power coursing through her veins. A vampire, she could sense a vampire. She could smell its fear as she pounced, her fangs sank into the flesh and hot liquid burst like berries in her mouth. She groaned and bit deeper. From far away she could hear someone calling but she needed more. She felt the body beneath her start to go limp.

'Hey!' A voice roared. Regina growled in anger. She turned blood dripping to the floor. The vampire whimpered and crawled away. Searing heat hit her, as fire struck her again and again. When the flames had cleared she found herself face to face with a Black dragon. It loomed above her, she heard Poppy scream… Poppy, where was Poppy? Where was she? What had she done? She shook the hunger from her mind and carefully put her monster away.

'What …?' She questioned circling the dragon. It had to be at least 20 feet tall or more. With leathery wings at its back. Giant scales bigger than dinner plates glistened up and down its body. She edged towards her friends, wincing as she saw Aurora cowering and clutching her throat.

'Ladies,' Dragmir announced. Nonchalantly stepping between them and the dragon. 'May I introduce Davina's alter ego … Baby.' The dragon bowed her head.

'That's … that's Davina?' Poppy stuttered.

'Sort of,' Dragmir said scratching his head as if he was struggling to explain it clearly, which, he was.

'No,' the dragon boomed. 'She is vampire, I am dragon. Sometimes we have to compromise on space, so one of us goes dormant.' She gave a skin crawling grin.

'How?' Imogen sputtered eventually.

'The price of being in The Darkness for so long,' Baby sighed. 'I am one of the oldest residents here. Most become The Lost, those who escape it … The Darkness consumes us and we are torn in two. The light and the dark.'

'So you're a manifestation of Davina's darker side.' Poppy stated. Baby laughed, a surprisingly light melodic sound.

'Oh goodness me no, I am her light. Davina is the one to be wary of.' Seeing the shocked looks, she sighed and rolled her enormous eyes. 'That's profiling in action.'

Baby folded her scaly black arms across her expanse of a chest, drumming her talons as if highly offended. Regina smirked and started to giggle. Imogen shot her a confused look. Baby looked severely affronted and turned muttering away to herself.

'I'm sorry Baby. I'm just relieved to meet another so called monster like myself, who seems to be anything but,' Regina explained through her relieved laughter. Imogen bit her lip, she had a habit of catching her friend's laughter at the most inopportune times. Baby seemed appeased by this and relented allowing another slightly less terrifying smile.

'So if we get stuck here …' Aurora gulped looking horrified, as if the impact had just fully hit her.

'You will most likely become Lost. There are few who can hold onto themselves and as you can see, they do not completely.' Baby flapped her wings sadly.

'How long do we have before we become Lost or change?' Regina asked worriedly, scared she would not like the answer.

'Those with little power are lost quite quickly. It seems that those who have the most power become like me … like Davina. Davina did something terrible …' Baby shuddered. 'Now she is as good as lost, I am all that remains of her goodness. When she is control, she thinks only of indulging herself no matter the consequence, no matter the number of casualties.' Regina swallowed hard, acutely aware that this could very well be her fate.

'We need to get out of here as soon as possible,' Imogen said eyeing Regina cautiously, she was obviously thinking the same thing. 'Is there a way?'

'There is, I saw Davina show a vampire and elf the

way. It will not be easy and I don't know how long I will be able to remain in control. So I can tell you how to get there but I must stay. If Davina regains control …' Baby trailed off.

'No!' Regina interrupted. 'You're coming with us. We can't leave you here, if we can get through to the Other Place so can you.' Aurora looked at her like she'd lost her mind.

'Regina's right. I have heard there is powerful magic in the Other Place. I think we could save Davina from herself,' Poppy mused thoughtfully. Baby perked at this thought. Her sea-green eyes glimmering with hope. 'Plus it must be handy to have a dragon on hand in this place,' she added. Aurora nodded dumbly. Her usual brash nature had all but retreated.

'I will have to allow Davina to return for a short time but I will be back for the journey.' She blinked her eyes sadly and took to the skies, leaving the others looking confused, their eyes cast skyward, to the murky expanse above.

'Come,' Dragmir snapped them from their reverie. 'We should rest. I will watch for Davina, she may return whilst we sleep. I will ensure no harm comes to you.' His voice washed over Regina and she gladly welcomed the chance to rest. The Darkness weighed on her heavily, she felt it changing her, crawling inside her skin, infecting her. Aurora clutched her throat and skittered quickly past Regina, her eyes wide with fear.

Regina escaped to Davina's bathroom, her eyes black in the mirror. It was taking control, she could feel it. Her thoughts strayed to Jay, her eyes closed trying to picture what he would make of all of this. He would probably have some corny pun about Baby the dragon, he would make her laugh, he would make her feel. The thought warmed her and as her eyes opened, she saw her own reflected back, but the thought of him did little to wash the blood from her hands and as she scrubbed Aurora's from them, her sobs came in earnest.

Chapter 6

The resistance

Sheeva arrived in a swirl of dark clouds and fog. The clouds had not stopped their weeping since Regina entered The Darkness, as though they knew she'd gone, taking all hope with her. Martha handed Sheeva a towel, lamenting the horrid climate. Sheeva and Thomas exchanged resigned knowing glances. They had spent the evenings since Regina left planning, they both knew it was not a coincidence. It was not merely the weather, the air around appeared to hold despair. Sheeva flexed her wings, drying them in the warm before they disappeared as if a mirage. Martha pulled a grumbling John out of the chair he appeared to have staked a claim on and said goodnight to Thomas and Sheeva, a mixture of excitement and dread in her eyes. Tomorrow they would infiltrate the Council, it could mean the end of hiding, running; it could mean everything.

'You think we have a chance?' Thomas asked. His blue eyes shone hopefully as he spoke. They were sat on the couch now, Sheeva's legs tucked beneath her as she blew onto her piping hot nettle tea. She shrugged.

'I really don't know, but I think you're right. We have to try. The longer they continue thinking that Regina killed Helena, the worse things will get for us. Eli has lost his way completely. His judgement is flawed where Helena is concerned and I fear once his search is complete he will turn his attention to rooting out the resistance.' Her black eyes hardened as she thought of all the good people who had joined the resistance to give their families a better future. They burned with tears as she remembered those Helena had ordered killed at the resistance headquarters, just to make a point.

'I still haven't managed to talk Martha out of coming along,' Thomas looked desperately at Sheeva. She observed Thomas curiously, wondering why he was suddenly so protective of Martha.

'She has her powers back now, does she not?' She asked placing her tea back down on the low white table before her. Thomas nodded in reply. 'I'm sure she will be fine. Besides, she will be with you and I know you will keep her safe,' Sheeva squeezed the old man's hand reassuringly.

'I'm sure you're right,' he mumbled. 'I just can't help feeling responsible for her and her family, after all she's the only family Regina has left, other than her mother.' He winced as he thought of the still woman above them, who had all but stopped breathing. Thomas wondered if her mother would still be alive, if Regina by some miracle did find her way back. He hoped against hope that she would, but he knew that was a pipedream at best.

'You know we all love Regina and I pray she makes it back, but you can't save everyone Thomas. You just can't.' Thomas sighed, his shoulders sagging and for a moment he felt as old as his illusion portrayed him to be. Sheeva's words did little to ease his heavy heart. Once again he was left with the feeling that no one knew him, not really and if they did … he just didn't deserve their pity.

'I think I'll have a turn around the garden before retiring for the night,' Thomas rose, patting Sheeva on the shoulder. 'You should get some sleep, we have a big day tomorrow.' He breezed out of the patio door and disappeared into the dark, leaving Sheeva puzzling over this conundrum of a man.

Morning came with cruel haste. Rays slid through the tree-line which surrounded the barn and shards of gold peeked through the kitchen window, illuminating Thomas' slouched figure. He wore the same crumpled clothes he had the night before Sheeva noted as she entered the room. As he turned his face in greeting, the shadows beneath his eyes told her he had not slept. For a second Sheeva started as Thomas' eyes flashed, changing colour, as if he was losing control and her breath caught. They reminded her of someone she had lost long ago, but before she had time to react they were back to their usual shape and colour. She shook the thought from her head and busied herself heating the potion she'd made the night before for Martha. The purple liquid bubbled and sparked when it reached the optimum temperature. Sheeva quickly removed it from the hob and poured it straight into a discoloured and chipped cauldron. She muttered a transformation spell and stirred in three sprigs of mint to make it more palatable.

Martha appeared as though summoned just as Sheeva was pouring the potion into a glass flask. John remained upstairs with the children. Martha had said her goodbyes the night before. She had told Thomas that she did not want to upset the children, but as Sheeva placed the flask in Martha's shaking hand, she had a feeling that the children's absence was more for Martha. She smiled brightly, but her eyes betrayed her as she drank the potion, switching from fear to hopelessness. Sheeva almost spoke her mind and told Martha to stay but she knew it was important for her, whether she feared what was to come or not. She had felt it since Thomas told her Martha would be coming and Sheeva learnt long ago that to go against her instincts, was to tempt fate. She would not make that mistake again. She thought of him in that second, just for a second. A flash of his smile, his deep voice calling her name. She blinked back her tears and smiled encouragingly at Martha, as she began to change slowly in appearance. A few minutes later, a svelte looking figure replaced that of the stout wife and mother. Martha had gained an inch or two in height and appeared younger than before. She inspected herself in the mirror, smiling and nodding in approval.

'Pity this can't be more permanent,' she said in a sultry Romanian accent, running her fingers through her now sleek, curl-free auburn hair. 'Much easier than trying to diet,' she giggled. Martha caught Thomas' eye in the reflection and mouthed an apology, chastising herself for being so flippant. Thomas frowned but Sheeva bit her lip to hide a grin, relieved that the icy atmosphere appeared to have thawed a little.

'Now,' Thomas said pacing across the thick rug before the hearth. 'Who are you?' He raised his brow. He was back to his old self now it seemed, all tiredness erased from his face. Strength and determination flowed from him despite his frail looking frame.

'My name is Honora Geltz. I am bodyguard to Vladimir Kruntez a foreign dignitary visiting from Romania. I have been in the country for just over a month and have met Eli Masters three times. I am married and have one child who is currently serving his apprenticeship under Peter Hughes, a wizard well known for his changeling abilities. I am a wand carrying witch and specialise in protection of politicians. I have worked for Vladimir for the past seven years. My husband is back in Romania where he sits on the local council of Elders, representing healer wizards in the area,' Martha rattled it all off quickly, her eyes far away as if ticking off a mental checklist in her head. Thomas nodded in approval.

'Once we arrive, I will request a meeting with Eli. Disguised as Vladimir, he will have no choice but to accept. Sheeva has informed me that he and Vladimir have certain interests in common. Namely that he would like to extend the reach of the death squads, as much as Eli does. Vladimir holds a lot of sway with the council and his vote of confidence in this will be invaluable to him.' Martha shuddered at the mention of the death squads, but Thomas seemed to pay no heed and continued running through their plan one more time. If this was to work, they all had to play their parts perfectly. If not, it could have deadly consequences. 'Sheeva can get us into the building and will accompany us into Eli's chambers. After that, it's down to us to convince him,' he finished, a look of readiness about him.

'What if he won't listen to reason?' Martha asked tucking her newly shiny hair behind her ear.

'If things go wrong use your wand to bring you back, being a bodyguard you are permitted to carry it which means you can travel in and out quickly. Sheeva can of course do this anyway being a nymph and I will have this,' Thomas held up a bottle containing a shimmering black powder.

'Is that cuniculum powder?' Martha marvelled. The Council were very particular about keeping tabs on the magical community and one of those ways was the banning of cuniculum production. She had seen it only once before when she was a child. She discovered it in her mother's healing supplies whilst playing with Evelyn one day. Their mother had berated them, telling them never to speak of seeing the powder again to another soul. Martha remembered it vividly, as it was one of the few times she had truly seen her mother angry. She hadn't understood at the time and cried in her room, while Evelyn soothed her and stroked her hair. Martha's previous doubts were beaten back by the humming now in her heart, a song of hope struck up by this memory of her family. She could not fail them this time. She turned to face Thomas and Sheeva, her face blazed with such determination that Thomas was taken aback. The intensity in her eyes reminded him so much of Regina, it shook away any misgivings.

'Let's go,' he said and they did.

Chapter 7

The Journey

Regina was feeling very human. She felt every ache, every blister, mostly she felt the thirst. It clawed at her throat and shook her monster awake. Poppy noticed the change in her friend and she and Imogen took turns watching for the tell-tale signs; her blackened eyes and silences. At which point one or both of them would chatter incessantly about Regina's mother, father, the resistance and Jay. It was usually met with growls of frustration, but after a few minutes Regina was back to herself. Aurora stuck close to Baby, typically gravitating towards power. Her eyes slid towards Regina every few minutes, as though checking she would not be attacked again.

They found a large cave to take shelter after Baby announced it would soon be nightfall. Baby took to the skies as she had the night before. This time Regina volunteered to keep watch along with Imogen. Regina really didn't want to be alone with her so-called friend, however she knew being alone with her thoughts was equally dangerous and so said nothing. She retreated to the cave opening, a large crevice lined with damp felt-like moss, savouring the cold bursts of air whistling through it.

'They're asleep,' Imogen offered, settling beside Regina and leaning against the wet wall.

'That was quick,' Regina mused.

'I thought you might need this.' Imogen passed a fresh bag of blood to her. Regina's eyes flashed hungrily as she eyed the prize before her. Her eyes met Imogen's, there was no spark there and shadows haunted her eyes.

'This is yours,' Regina threw the bag back.

'You need it more,' Imogen argued.

'Becoming a martyr won't change what you've done. Did you really think a bag of blood would make things right between us?' Regina marched to the opposite side of the cave, her eyes blazing. She knew she needed to keep her temper in check, but Imogen being so close to her was making it hard to think clearly.

'I don't expect you to forgive me. I expect you to grow up, stop pouting, stop pretending that your dark side isn't surfacing and take the bloody bag … no pun intended,' Imogen tossed the bag at Regina and stormed out of the cave into the night.

'WAIT!' Regina called running after her. 'Come back in Immy. The Lost are out there. It's not safe.' She looked frantically around. She knew she shouldn't care. In fact, her monster screamed at her to stay silent, let her storm off and wander towards her own doom. The dull thrum of The Lost buzzed in the distance. 'Please!' Regina pleaded, her voice thick with heart-break at the thought of losing anyone else. She grabbed Imogen's hand, pulling her swiftly through the cave, just as a swarm of The Lost swept past.

'Thanks,' she choked out. 'I hate that you hate me,' Imogen finally managed as they listened to The Lost disappear into the distance. 'I don't blame you. I just hate us not being us, you know?' Regina nodded and she fought back the urge to throw her arms around her friend.

'I just can't forgive what you did. You understand don't you? You pretended to be someone you weren't. I opened up to you, I trusted you completely. I literally put my life and my parent's lives in your hands. Now my dad is rotting away in here, probably one of those things out there and god knows what will become of my mum. You were going to use me, just like Helena.' Regina's eyes shone, her cheeks damp with tears. 'That isn't even the worst part of it. I know that it should be, but what hurts most is that the 'us' that I miss, was never real. You were never my friend. You were Helena's lackey, just doing as you were told. At least Aurora is up-front about being an evil cow, you just pretended not to be one.' Imogen took it all, each word like a nail in the coffin of their friendship. She wondered if she should explain how she was misled by Helena. If she should tell her that they had been tortured within an inch of death and neither she nor her parents would tell Helena where she could be hiding. That she had ALWAYS been herself with Regina and that it wasn't a lie. One look at Regina told her, now was not the time. She was still grieving her father and this place appeared to have her trapped in a darker place than usual. No. She would get out of this, she would make things right and if that meant for now Regina had to hate her, she would have to bear it. Even if it tore her apart inside. The silence stretched out between them and Imogen watched a myriad of emotions run across her friends face.

'Well isn't this lovely,' Davina interrupted, appearing through the cave entrance, wearing a secret smile that made Regina shift uncomfortably. 'Old friends catching up on the good old days. You know Imogen, the ones where you stabbed her in the back and made her look like

67

a fool.' A wide satisfied grin spread across her face as Imogen rose and stomped back towards the others, muttering something about checking on Aurora.

'Good riddance I say,' Davina stated, inspecting her long black talon-like nails, before stroking her ruby curls with them.

'What would you know about it?' Regina accused.

'You're right of course,' she said in an almost humble, very un-Davina-like way. 'I don't know the particulars, but I do know what it feels like to be let down by someone you love. To put your trust in them, your very life and for them to betray you.' Her hands balled in fists at her side, her talons drawing blood as she did.

'Doesn't that hurt?' Regina pointed to her bloodied hands.

'Not at all,' Davina held her already healing palms out for Regina to inspect.

'But how? I thought we lost our healing abilities in this place?'

'There are ways,' Davina said simply, smoothing her hands over her black velvet corset and fingering her heavy crimson skirt absently.

'How?' Regina asked. If she could feed and heal, maybe she could keep The Darkness at bay a little longer. Davina walked to the opening and crooked a finger at Regina.

'Come little one,' she whispered before stepping out. Regina bit her lip, casting her eyes toward the back of the cave, before following; only to find herself alone. 'Up here,' Davina called. Regina looked upwards, Davina hovered not far above her head. Regina gasped, it felt like the first time she had seen a vampire fly all over again, this should be impossible, flight was impossible in here. They had all tried. Poppy could barely manage to flit between her normal and smaller size and even that was becoming harder.

'How?' Regina breathed almost silently as Davina landed gracefully next to her.

'I feed on The Lost.'

'But how can you? One of them touched me and I was in agony.' Regina shook her head.

'Once you have fed on The Lost, you will be immune to their touch,' Davina said simply.

'So if I feed on The Lost, I'll be able to heal, use my abilities and The Lost won't affect me?' Regina observed Davina carefully. Baby had warned her about Davina's darkness, but this seemed like a perfect solution. If she could keep her monster at bay a little longer, she would be less afraid of losing control. 'What's the catch?' Regina questioned.

'No catch. You need to feed and I don't fancy being cooped up with a murderous monster.' That made sense. Baby said that Davina would always put herself first. She pondered for a moment, what could be the harm? As long as she could feed and stay herself it was worth the risk. Regina nodded and Davina led her through the crooked trees towards The Lost.

'See that one?' Davina said as she crouched behind a tree, pointing toward one of The Lost. It appeared to be a man, he was swaying and staring at his hands, whilst the others hungrily scanned the woods for souls to claim. 'He's newly Lost.' Regina looked confused, Davina continued. 'When they are first taken they really are lost, they aren't quite as quick as the others and haven't figured out how to fight as effectively. Those are the ones we hunt. They are easy to lure away, easy to catch and they still have a tiny piece of their soul which makes them more … palatable.' Regina winced at her choice of words, but needs must. Davina moved toward The Lost, careful to stay out of view of the others. The Lost man looked up, stunned for a moment by the sight of Davina. Regina didn't blame him, she was stunning and terrifying all at the same time. He gazed at Davina as though entranced and she laughed softly licking her lips before dashing back behind the tree where Regina waited. Her head spun, she knew she couldn't kill him, he was already dead, but this felt wrong. She couldn't, she wouldn't.

'Quit your belly aching, we're hungry.' Regina gasped, her monster hadn't spoken to her in so long, not since she had first begun to change, when she had no control. *'Do I have to do everything myself?'* Her monster snapped.

'Regina, are you alive?' Davina shook her hard. Her eyes flickered open, she lay in a pile of ash and dust in the woods. Davina rolled her eyes impatiently.

'What happened? The last thing I remember, you were leading that soul toward me.' Regina's brow furrowed as she tried to remember anything. Davina laughed, the kind of laughter reserved for those moments in life when you know a delicious secret. Regina jumped to her feet, she felt strong, she felt … normal, well normal for her.

'You mean you don't remember doing that?' Davina pointed to what seemed to be more ash and leaves. Regina moved in for a closer look and nearly gagged. The Lost soul from the wood had been torn limb from limb, his insides strewn across the cracked and dusty wooded floor. For a moment the world spun and Regina struggled to remain upright.

'I didn't … I could never…' but even as the words formed on her lips she knew it was true. Flashes of her ripping into his soft flesh arose in her mind. She raised her fingers to her lips, she could still taste him. She remembered drinking him till he was nearly spent and then, something even darker had taken hold, something at her core, it had finally clawed its way free. She had slashed and torn till there was nothing left of him. The sick feeling rose again and dark pools of blood spewed from her mouth, she bent over clutching her knees, heaving and taking deep shuddering breaths. Davina looked on unruffled by the scene, examining her talons once more.

'What a waste, never mind you still have enough in your system to keep you going. If you've finished with your emotional breakdown, we need to get back, it's almost morning and my scaly friend will be kicking me out soon enough,' Davina grumbled coldly. Pouting at the inconvenience Baby caused her, no thought for the Lost soul or Regina. She took to the sky and after a few more deep breaths Regina joined her, both exhilarated to be flying again and saddened by the cost.

I told you I'd take care of it,' her monster growled. Regina had a feeling that she had just made everything much worse.

D M Singh

Chapter 8

Into the belly of the beast

The Council of Elders chamber's was nestled amongst the tower blocks and offices in the centre of London; hiding in plain sight. Sheeva led the way quickly through the darkened streets, Martha and Thomas hurrying to keep up. Martha tried to take in her surroundings as they hurried but they moved so quickly it was a blur. She had been to London only once before but she had barely been a toddler at the time and remembered nothing of it.

It was after 8am and the streets were filling with workers jostling along, coffee cups in hand eager to be out of the dampening, chilly air. The sky was even darker today Martha noticed as if even the heavens knew something was coming. She shook the thought away.

'This way quickly,' Sheeva urged. They squeezed through the crumbling doorway of what appeared to be a book shop. It was hard to tell if it was in fact a book shop, as the windows were covered in a film of brown grime, preventing anyone from looking in or out. Once inside it was apparent that this was not a book shop – Indeed it was not. Martha stood agape. All around witches, wizards, vampires, werewolves, elves, nymphs, even giants and a few unicorns were rushing to work just like the humans were outside. Martha wondered how they ever kept this a secret.

'You've been here before remember Honora,' Thomas

whispered through his barely moving lips. 'Try not to act like a tourist.' Martha snapped out of her daze, embarrassed. 'Show time,' he grinned. Martha relaxed and nodded. She flanked Thomas, wand in hand and walked confidently through the crowd, all the time checking her peripheral vision for threats. Sheeva hurried beside her looking pleased. She carried the files containing the evidence they had gathered so far against Helena. They approached a hall lined with guards, most of them members of the Death Squad. Eli had called half their number back to protect the council, whilst the other half searched for Helena. Sheeva tensed as they passed, worried Martha would be undone by the soldiers who had tortured and killed her parents but she played her part to perfection. Her head held high, eyes cold and fierce as she passed them by. Sheeva felt a surge of admiration for this brave woman who had lost just as much as Regina, yet here she was heading into the belly of the beast, brave and fearless as her niece.

At the end of the hallway Eli's assistant rose from his chair, a fake smile plastered on his werewolf face. Sheeva wore her own fake smile, a genuine one would not surface for him. Julian was a yes man, anything Eli said was gospel to him and he worshipped Eli like he was some kind of Messiah. His simpering ways always made Sheeva's skin crawl, but she had kept her revulsion well-hidden thus far and she was not about to slip.

'Vladimir has requested to speak with Eli,' Sheeva said as she reached his desk. Julian looked perplexed for a moment and furrowed his brow whilst rummaging through a diary in front of him.

'I don't have anything on the books,' Julian replied in

his nasally voice.

'I'm sure Eli will want to take this meeting,' Sheeva insisted, her voice raised in impatience. Thomas caught her eye and shook his head, she bit her lip and regained control, smiling once more at Julian.

'Eli has left specific orders not to be disturbed. By anyone,' Julian glowered at Sheeva. A growl originating in Julian's chest echoed through the hallway and she cursed herself for forgetting it was almost the full moon, which always left him in an uncooperative mood. Sheeva was just considering the best way to placate him, when Martha stepped forward, her wand pointed at Julian's throat and a deadly look in her eyes.

'I think you'll find Vladimir's name in your book,' she hissed. Julian snarled in response.

'Fine!' Martha said shrugging. 'Have it your way wolf boy but when I see Eli, I'll be sure to tell him that you were the one who prevented him from finding Helena.' Julian looked terrified at the thought of being on the receiving end of Eli's rage.

'You know where she is?' He asked uncertainly. He did not seem completely convinced.

'Of course I don't you imbecile, I'm merely a bodyguard, but he,' she gestured to Thomas, who stood head held high with an arrogant look of distaste on his face, 'says that he does and I would not like to argue with him. I've seen first-hand what happens to those who do not see things his way.' Martha gave a knowing smile, it was strangely cold and menacing. The whole time this interaction had taken place, Martha's wand remained trained on Julian's throat, her hand steady.

'I think I did see your name on the books my Lord. My

mistake, my writing really is terrible.' Julian proclaimed holding up the book before quickly snapping it shut. 'Go right in my Lord,' he bowed as he spoke.

'Wise choice,' Martha hissed as she passed the werewolf and Sheeva grinned, noting never to cross Martha.

'I THOUGHT I TOLD YOU NOT TO DISTURB ME?' Eli screamed as Sheeva pushed open the heavy doors. Eli flushed immediately seeing Vladimir. Vladimir was easily one of the most powerful vampires in the world, bar Helena. His word carried a lot of sway with the rest of the council. It would not do for him to quarrel with Vladimir, he needed his support now more than ever. 'Vladimir my dear friend. I am so sorry. I thought you were that moronic wolf,' he beamed as he crossed the room to shake his hand. 'To what do I owe the honour of this visit?' He gestured to an easy chair near the fire. Martha waved her wand and conjured another chair for Sheeva. She took her place by the door, wand drawn and at the ready. Sheeva took her seat, silently wondering if Martha had missed her calling in life. Thomas coughed loudly, whilst Martha flicked her wrist, locking the door.

'I have most urgent information regarding the whereabouts of the girl and Helena,' his heavily accented voice drawled. Eli sat up eagerly in his chair. Thomas closed his eyes and a moment later the illusion of Vladimir had shimmered away leaving Thomas sat opposite the man responsible for the death of hundreds of resistance members. It took all of his strength not to leap across the desk and kill him with his bare hands. Thomas gritted his teeth, he knew Eli could not be touched. If people were to believe that the resistance truly meant no harm and that Regina had been persecuted wrongly, the murdering snake had to remain in one piece. Eli's mouth hung open for a second, before a look of surprise turned to confusion and then anger.

'Who are you?' He bellowed, leaping to his feet, wand drawn.

'Eli, this is Thomas. The leader of the resistance,' Sheeva stated. She was on her feet too now. Her hands up in surrender, she knew how quickly he could lose his temper. They could not afford for this to go wrong. They had just exposed Thomas, who had managed to stay off the grid for over fifteen years.

'I don't understand,' Eli growled at Sheeva, but his eyes remained on the old man who sat, quite at ease it appeared in his office. 'Did you capture him? Why didn't you contact me or my captain? The death squad could have handled this, why the theatrics?'

'I assure you Eli. I am no-one's prisoner,' Thomas said calmly.

'Traitor!' Eli seethed. His eyes filled with violent promises were now fixed on Sheeva, someone he had come to trust implicitly over the years.

'Hear him out Eli,' Sheeva said, her eyes on the door. Eli pondered this for moment.

'You have one minute,' he snapped, his fingers drumming on the desk.

'Like I said before I know where Helena is and I have information about Regina.' Eli observed him suspiciously through beady eyes. 'Helena is not dead, Regina has not harmed her in any way. I'm afraid Helena has deceived you,' he threw the file onto the desk in front of Eli, who swiftly picked it up and scoured the pages with haste.

'What is this?' He barked, face red with rage. Holding up the file Regina had found in the old manor house. It read like a private investigators report, tracking Regina's movements over the years. He thrust the file at Thomas. 'All this proves, is that you are just as big a danger to our community as the girl you hide,' he narrowed his eyes, brows drawn together in anger. 'You knew where she was all along,' he accused. 'You have put us all in danger, because you do not have the guts to do what needs to be done.'

'You're right,' Thomas placated. Sheeva looked confused. 'I have always known where Regina was, I have watched over her all these years. I have seen her grow from a chubby cheeked toddler into a fine young woman, however this research is not mine. This belongs to Helena. She has always known Regina's location.' Eli shook his head as though shaking the thought free.

'No, you're wrong,' he spat, 'Helena would never … she could not do that.' He sounded uncertain and enraged at once.

'It's true,' Sheeva said. 'We found this at her country manor. She sent some of her most loyal followers to retrieve the girl. She hoped to use Regina and her power to overthrow you and the council.' Sheeva waited while Eli processed this. His face a mask of pain and anguish.

'NO!' Eli shouted so suddenly that Martha started, gripping her wand tighter. 'No, it's lies,' he flung the file to the floor like a child throwing a tantrum.

'Eli,' Sheeva said gently. 'I know it sounds crazy, but I have seen it with my own eyes. Helena hid Regina from you and when Regina refused to join her, she killed her father, injured her mother and fled into The Darkness.' Eli looked incredulous at this. His face paled for a second.

'Emile is dead? ... and Evelyn she is ...' He trailed off looking empty and lost. Sheeva nodded, she knew that Evelyn's father had been close friends with Eli once. He swallowed hard.

'How do I know you are telling me the truth? Even if what you say about Helena is right, that does not mean that Regina is innocent. You are resistance and here you sit bold as brass in my chambers. You would say anything to further your cause and save your own hides.' He looked conflicted and Sheeva felt a surge of hope tugging at her heart. Perhaps this would work.

'I have no reason to lie and I am not resistance,' Martha piped up. Sheeva handed her a potion and she drank, her illusion shedding as the liquid was ingested.

'Impossible,' Eli breathed, eyes wide in shock as the daughter of his old friend appeared before him.

'You remember me then?' Martha hissed. 'Look I'm a little late to this ... party. Up until a few days ago, I thought I was a normal mortal. My mother hid me before...' She shuddered but then continued, 'all I know is Regina saved me from Helena, she saved my children, my husband. She is NOT what we all thought she would be. We were wrong.' Eli considered this scratching his chin, his eyes far away. The atmosphere was palpable, as the man who had the power to bring this to an end and help them try and bring Regina back deliberated this information.

'We, you said we were wrong, but what you meant was, I was wrong,' his voice though soft, had an unnerving edge to it that made Sheeva feel ill at ease. Nobody spoke. What could they say? He was the one who had started all of this with his witch hunt. He had the power to help his old friend when he came to him for protection, instead he had used it as a platform to secure still more power. He had signed the order for Regina's grandparents, parents and any family members to be questioned. Which in the Death squad's eyes was an open invitation to torture and kill.

Eli moved swiftly from behind the desk his wand drawn, his hand steady, he kept it trained on Thomas. Martha raised her wand but Thomas shook his head.

'We've given Eli enough to think about,' Sheeva said sensing the sudden change in the room's atmosphere. 'We'll leave these with you,' she indicated the now scattered file. Eli snarled, picked the file and loose sheaves of paper and threw them into the fireplace. Martha gasped in shock.

'Why would you do that?' Thomas said, only slightly perplexed as though he knew what the answer to be already.

'The people need a strong leader, a decisive leader, one to make hard choices. That's me, I do that every day no matter the cost. You people walk around so high and mighty, you think you can save everyone. Well you can't. Sacrifices need to be made for the greater good in any society and I have done that. That … monster is the reason my oldest friend is dead, she is the reason Emile is dead; she is the problem here. This wild theory of yours will never leave this room,' His face menacing, as he rounded on them.

'You think burning a few bits of paper will stop this from getting out?' Martha said in disbelief. 'Once people know the truth ….'

'Oh, you misunderstand me Martha. When I say your theory will never leave this room. I meant you'll never leave this room.' No sooner had the words left his mouth, then the door flew open and two soldiers stormed in.

'Go!' Thomas cried as he tackled Eli. Martha flicked her wand sending one of the soldiers skidding across the room, into a large bookcase, which teetered before tipping over. Hefty volumes connected with the soldier, who grunted in pain and seemed momentarily dazed. Sheeva fired stunners from her fingertips, which the soldier dodged. He lunged forwards to grab the nymph but she quickly shrank to her diminutive form and he landed in a heap on the carpet.

'I SAID GO!' Thomas bellowed as he struggled with Eli.

'No, I'm not leaving you,' Sheeva yelled back, landing an impressive roundhouse kick on a shocked soldier, who crumpled before quickly regrouping.

'Right behind you,' he shouted, retrieving the bottle of Cuniculum powder. Martha muttered a spell and flicked her wand disappearing first. Sheeva followed but not before she saw Eli wrestle the bottle from Thomas' hand and hit him with a spell. Thomas crumpled to the floor, his eyes on Sheeva as she disappeared, arms outstretched, calling his name.

D M Singh

Chapter 9
House bound

Regina managed to reach the cave before dawn. Davina had already left, it appeared both she and Baby did not like to have an audience when they changed. Luckily Imogen had fallen asleep, probably because she hadn't fed since they arrived. Regina had a feeling she was still holding onto the bag of blood for her and she felt a pang of guilt, she felt no hunger, instead she felt better than she had in a long time. She watched as Imogen stretched and groaned at her aching muscles. Imogen was so busy trying to apologise for abandoning her post, that it was completely lost on her that Regina had been gone all night. How could she be so selfish? Regina's chest ached at the thought, she had left them unprotected to feed herself.

'*We'll be more careful next time*,' her monster assured, she shook her head.

'There won't be a next time,' she hissed. Imogen sighed looking worn, assuming Regina's mistrust of her had grown even more over-night. Regina bit her lip to stop herself telling Imogen it wasn't her fault, she wanted to tell her she was fine, that she could drink the blood herself. But her monster snatched the words from her before they formed.

Baby arrived with an earth trembling thud outside the cave and dust swirled around them as they stepped out into the ebony hue of day. The beating of Baby's wings nearly knocking Aurora on her backside, which elicited a wicked looking smile from Poppy. Her eyes danced excitedly in a way that made Regina feel strange. Was this place beginning to affect her too? They needed to get out of here and soon.

They had been walking for the better part of a day when Baby finally managed to get Regina alone. Regina had avoided her as long as she could, scared she knew, scared she would tell the others, that they would think they were wrong to believe in her goodness, that she was indeed a monster.

'You know?' Regina asked but she already knew the answer and lowered her eyes in shame.

'I see all she sees,' Baby said. Regina grimaced at this. It was bad enough that she had given into her urges but for Baby to have seen her like that made her feel sick all over again. 'I should have warned you. This is my fault. I knew Davina fed on The Lost. I just never imagined she would share that with you. I'm sorry.' Regina looked up into the giant creature's guilt-ridden eyes, confused.

'You have nothing to be sorry for. No-one forced me to go into those woods, not even Davina. I thought if I could just curb my hunger, that I could hang onto my humanity a little longer. I thought it might keep you all safe longer. I was so scared of what I thought I was turning into, but by doing this I've only hastened my way along the dark path,' Regina let a slow breath out. It was hard but she was glad to share this with someone who actually seemed to care about her. 'We can't tell the others.' Regina's eyes pleaded with the dragon, who simply nodded in agreement.

'I agree, no good can come of sharing this information,'

Baby said quietly. The others had gone ahead and since their senses had all been dulled to that of a human in this place, they could speak freely.

'What did she do?' Regina asked. Baby looked quizzical. 'Davina,' she clarified, 'you said that before she split into … her and you she did a terrible thing.' Baby stopped walking and hung her head, her eyes filled with pain.

'We were one then. When it happened. Things were scary but we managed. We fed on The Lost but never to excess and we took no pleasure in it. I remember we had been here for a long time, I'm not sure how long. We were desperate for a way through to the other place. There was someone there we loved very much. We were desperate to see him. It clawed at our mind, we needed him, but we were trapped. For a long time we tried everything we could to get through. Then we discovered there was a way through but it would only open for one particular person. One neither alive nor dead, he could pass through, then the way through would close. His love would follow the same as he, neither alive nor dead only then would the way through open completely. We thought it was us. So we found an old witch who knew the way, the price she asked for her services was high. I didn't want to do it, but the part of me which is now Davina wanted him back at any cost.' She paused and shuddered as though every syllable cost her a part of her soul. 'The old witch wanted children from the mortal world. I don't know what for, all I knew is that she wanted us to kill children. She had a spell which would send us back to inhabit a body for a short amount of time. She cast it, even though I refused and said I would find another way. The child she sent us for was barely ten years old, as soon as we saw him, we knew we could never do what she asked, but we were hungry. We had been in The Darkness for so very long and we finally had a body ...' she trailed off as giant tears rolled down her scaly cheek. 'It had been such a long time since we had fed, we underestimated how much we could take, it was too much. He was dead in seconds. Then we were back here again. The witch showed us the way but told us we were not the one who would open it. It had all been for nothing. We sat in the dark for weeks, barely moving torn between rage and guilt, eventually we became two. I held all the guilt, sorrow and goodness and Davina ... she thinks only of revenge on the witch and on the one who trapped us here.' No-one spoke for a long time, they moved quietly. Regina's heart swelled with sorrow for this kind creature and even for Davina, could she really blame her for losing it in this place? She had been here centuries, with no-one, no purpose, no hope. She had only been here a short time and she was already losing her way. Could she really point the finger at anyone?

'What is that?' Aurora squeaked, coming to a halt.

'That is the seam,' Baby answered. In the distance a purple tinge of light flickered and flashed, bursts of lightening streaked above them, illuminating the path. In the light Regina watched as a woman near the seam reached for it hopefully, only to be incinerated in an instant. Imogen cried out in horror, Poppy looked away tears in her eyes.

'We're going through there?' Regina asked, hoping she was wrong. Baby nodded. 'What happens if ... you know ... that happens. Could that happen?'

'It's a possibility. However given that Helena managed to pass through, I think we have a good chance. We need to find shelter for the night. We should not try cross at night, we don't know what's waiting on the other side.'

'I know a place not far from here,' Dragmir said, his eyes scanning the horizon. 'It's been a long time, but if I remember correctly, it's just a few minutes from here. He took the path to the left, before laughing and heading in the opposite direction.

'Doesn't exactly fill you with confidence, does he?' Poppy laughed skipping after him.

To their surprise Dragmir found a house. Something they had not yet come across. From the little they had seen of The Darkness thus far, those who lived here had forged their homes in tree, caves, underground, but here it stood. Front garden, complete with a bright red swing. It looked like one of the old Victorian stone-built terrace houses Regina had lived in as a toddler, yet it stood alone. Regina couldn't explain why, but this house made her uneasy. They approached the door, past the still swinging, swing. Dragmir pushed the door hesitantly, before turning to beckon the others. After a few moments lingering in the dusty hallway, Regina climbed the stairs, excited by the prospect of a little normalcy.

There were four large bedrooms, each with large double beds and a bathroom with a bath so dirty it looked black.

'There are beds up here,' Regina called down the stairs, seconds later there was a thundering of feet as they argued over who would have to share with whom. A string with a wood teardrop at one end, hung at the end of the hallway. Regina pulled and heavy, wooden steps clattered down.

The steps groaned and grumbled as she climbed them carefully. She whispered to the air and orbs illuminated the room. It appeared to be an old playroom or nursery. An old doll house sat beneath the windowsill, a rocking horse laced with cobwebs bobbed back and forth in the corner. Boxes and trunks over-flowing with toys littered the floor. In the shadows of the furthest corner she thought she saw her own eyes staring back at her and gasped.

'Reggie,' a voice called from the shadows, a voice she knew, a voice she had thought she would never hear again.

'Dad?' She clamped a hand over her mouth as tears fell thick and fast. Out of the shadows stepped Emile Vasilescu, a look of surprise on his face. He was across the room in a second and swept Regina into his arms. She sobbed, wretched soul shaking sobs. He pulled back, staring into her eyes as he wiped her tears away with his thumbs.

'How are you here?' She wondered, still clinging to him.

'I heard the rumour about the seam and a vampire who was dragging a reluctant half-elf with her through The Darkness, plus I had help. An inside man feeding me information, well technically a woman.' Regina looked confused, who could be here and in the mortal world? Her face lit as she realised the only person it could be.

'Mum?' She squeaked. 'Where is she?' She spun looking around excitedly.

'She's still alive and since her body has not passed on, she cannot be here all of the time. She comes and goes. She told me Jay had been taken into The Darkness and so naturally we assumed you would go charging after him, no thought for yourself.' Regina reddened, waiting for the lecture about being more careful, it didn't come. Instead he beamed at her with pride.

'Wait, you're not mad? Is Mum?'

'Of course we're not mad sweetheart. You're very much like us you know and though we worry about you, we understand. Besides, I would have done the same thing. So would your mother, though she would never admit it.'

'You have to come with us dad, through to the other place. Maybe we can figure out a way to get you home,' Regina pleaded.

'Well of course I'm coming. What do you think I've been doing … waiting for you,' he grinned and Regina sighed happily, her chest felt a little less empty as she did.

'Wait till the others see you. They said you might be here, but they thought you'd become one of The Lost.' She bit her lip feeling ashamed that she hadn't made more of an effort to seek him out.

'You can thank your mother for keeping me safe. You know how scary she can be when she's in one of her moods, well even The Lost know better than to mess with her,' he laughed. 'Come on let's go scare the others half to death.' He grinned like a school boy and bounded down the steps making ghost sounds as he did.

D M Singh

Chapter 10

Captive

Time meant nothing. Shadows fell and moved across the tiny room, reaching the corners and the door; never escaping. Silence, chilling and unending stole after the shadows, returning when no escape would be found. So they remained captive, the three of them. The shadows, silence and Thomas.

Thomas was shocked at first that he had not been restrained, but after a few days he realised that the room had been spelled. Thomas could not perform any magic beyond his abilities as a changeling. Appealing to Eli's humanity and common sense had always been a long shot, but it was a calculated risk that had to be taken. If the attempt had been successful it would have prevented all-out war, which Thomas knew deep down was now unavoidable. He winced as he stood, his legs felt leaden and stiff, suddenly feeling as old as he appeared to be.

Though he was pleased that Sheeva and Martha had managed to escape Eli's clutches, Thomas knew that Sheeva would not let his incarceration stand. He also knew that Eli would now try and eliminate them all in order to keep the truth from getting out.

The gun-metal grey door screeched and creaked open and light spilled through. Thomas blinked rapidly in response and the narrow frame of the door was filled by a severe looking Eli Masters.

'You made a huge mistake coming here Thomas. Is that even your real name?' He questioned. The door scraped across the floor behind him setting Thomas' teeth on edge. Thomas remained silent, cursing how weak he felt right now. He was unfamiliar with the spell being used against him, but it was extremely clever. Eli knew that he would want to keep his guise in-tact and had left him enough power to maintain the illusion, but doing so was physically draining. Thomas had never felt so weak. Even standing left him short of breath. If it wasn't so cruel, Thomas would have been astonished by its simplicity and effectiveness. He knew he would not last long in his weakened state. Eli was holding all the cards right now and it sickened Thomas right down to his stomach. 'You will talk Thomas. They always do. I will know all about your shabby resistance members and I will hunt them down like the putrid, filthy traitors they are and I will crush each and every one of them,' Eli's voice rumbled like menacing thunder, his words extinguishing hope.

'They don't ALL talk though, do they Eli? Ernest and Hortence, they didn't talk did they?' Eli's face paled to near ivory at the mention of Regina's Grandparents, his oldest friends whom he had betrayed. Thomas grinned maliciously, enjoying the flash of pain in Eli's eyes. 'From what I heard, they never once buckled. Even after you'd lost your nerve and left the Death Squad to take over. How long did you torture the man who you lived with side by side as an apprentice?' Thomas' voice shook with emotion but never lost its timbre of authority. Even Eli's tricks couldn't change who he was. Eli turned, yanked the door open and strode down the hallway, leaving a surprised looking vampire to close the cell door.

Thomas let out a shaky breath and made it to the small bed before his legs gave out. He had rattled Eli, but he would regroup and return. He'd bought Sheeva a little time, but he knew they didn't have much. As his eyes gave up the ghost and fluttered shut, he thought of Sheeva and hoped that she had a plan to get him out before all hell broke loose.

Had it been weeks? Thomas drifted in and out, trying to organise his thoughts. He tried to focus on what he remembered. He definitely recalled coming to the Council of Elders to talk to Eli, but then… nothing. Had he come here with Regina? That had been the plan after all. If so, where was she? His eyes strained in the dark.

'Regina?' He croaked shakily. Nothing, no movements other than his own. Did Eli have her? Where was Sheeva? Pain shot though his head down his spine. His illusions were killing him, he could feel it. He needed to get out before his illusions failed him completely. Once Eli knew who he was, who he really was … he had to get out. He ground his teeth in determination, pulling himself up as every fibre in his body cried out in agony, but not a single sound left him as he struggled up. Thomas' long fingers grasped the handle of the door, locked. Of course it would be, although he was so confused right now, he could not remember if he had already tried the door. He paced, trying to think.

'Think, think, think…' He growled to himself as he fought against the change he could feel coming over his body. He concentrated, gathering every ounce of magic he could feel in his veins and the illusion slipped back into place. It would buy him a few days at the most.

'Feeling better are we?' Eli's voice washed over Thomas and he jumped. Where was it coming from? He spun around, he was alone. Was he finally going mad? 'No Thomas, you've not gone mad quite yet, but I would say you're well on your way,' Eli hissed.

'Come out you coward,' Thomas shouted. His eyes were filled with fury as they continued to search the room for his invisible foe. Manic laughter echoed all around him and Thomas swung his arms out, flailing in the darkness. His chest heaved and ached with the effort until every breath felt like tiny daggers piercing his heart.

'The sooner you tell me where they all are, this stops.'

Thomas shook his head resolutely, even this sent slices through his chest and body, causing him to scream out in pain.

'Never,' it came out as barely a whisper but Eli appeared to have heard regardless.

'Such a pity Thomas. I guess we do this the hard way.' Thomas cried out as the throbbing in his head turned to agony. He felt warm blood trickle from his ears. Tears rolled down his cheeks as he struggled to keep himself in check, he could not afford to give anything away. Despite the fact he did not know what was happening to him, if he was losing his mind or if he would even survive this, he did know one thing and that was he would never ever give up the resistance to Eli. He would die before that happened and that was his last thought before the world went black.

★ ★ ★ ★ ★ ★ ★ ★ ★ ★ ★ ★ ★ ★ ★ ★

The sun dropped below the hills which dotted the land

surrounding the safe house, the light slipping behind the hills as though running from whatever hid beyond the horizon. Amongst the tranquil scenery, the drums of war were beating, rumbles from a seemingly abandoned ruin of a barn. They had arrived over the last three days, careful they were not followed. Elf's, werewolves, vampires, nymphs, witches, wizards, even a troll had joined the assembly. Sheeva made some modifications to the barn with Martha and John's help. There was simply not enough room for all those who had heeded the SOS after their attempt to convince Eli to listen to reason. So the living room grew to twice its size, the kitchen multiplied its appliances. Two of everything appeared overnight, two ovens, two fridges, even the food doubled. Another floor sprung up enabling them to accommodate the travel weary visitors. Armchairs in the study blossomed into sofas. It seemed even the tumble down safe house had been enlisted in the resistance.

Sheeva greeted all the guests graciously, a smile of encouragement planted firmly on her face. Weaving through the many bodies mingling, eating and murmuring in the hallway, Sheeva made her way to the small bathroom, locking the door behind her. Her hands shook as she scooped cold water from the sink splashing her face, studying it. Her eyes were reddened and puffy from when she'd succumbed to panic during the night and wept, something she had not done for many years. The loss of Thomas had hit her harder than she cared to admit, the old man had grown on her and something in his eyes had always assured her that the resistance would be victorious. Now it fell to her; the thought froze her to the wooden floor of the tiny bathroom. Sheeva had never shied from leadership, she knew the Council Chambers better than anyone so it made sense she should be the one. Patting her face with a towel, Sheeva emerged, her confident smile in position.

'Shall we?' Sheeva said as she ushered the crowd towards the open plan living area, which was thankfully now big enough to accommodate. 'Has everyone arrived?' Sheeva took her place in the centre of the room, flicking her hand towards a chunky coffee table, which promptly walked out of the room, dodging legs as it went. Martha nodded in reply. 'As you have all heard by now, Thomas was captured in an attempt to persuade Eli of Regina's innocence and the truth behind who Helena really is.' She looked around the room seeing confused faces. Martha, John and both sets of twins were hurriedly passing out packets of research to those assembled. There was a rustling of papers, followed by some gasps and angry whispers. 'I know that you will have questions,' Sheeva said.

'Damn right we do,' shouted Gabriella. A vampire Sheeva recognised as one of the founding members of the resistance who had successfully infiltrated the guard of the Council of Elders. She went by Gabby now and she lived up to the name. For someone who lived a precise military-like life for such a long time, she had little love for authority. She was a valuable intelligence officer, but she also had a habit of stirring trouble. Gabby stood as some of the others tore their eyes from the information they had been given to hear what was being said. Gabby smiled as she slowly took in the room enjoying all eyes on her.

'I realise this is a lot to take in but for now we must

concentrate our efforts on rescuing Thomas.' There was a general murmur of assent as Sheeva spoke. Gabby however, was in full flow and shook her head, bouncing impatiently from toe to toe.

'Why?' She demanded. Confused looks, some of horror met her. 'He's a soldier just like any of us. He knew the risks going in, he's no more valuable than me, or Martha or you Sheeva.' Gabby was in her element as a few people grumbled in agreement.

'He is more important though ...'

Before Sheeva could finish gabby attacked, 'Oh that's rich. Yes he was our leader, yes he started this movement but why should we risk more of our number to save him? We are few in number as it is, if we were to attack the council how many of us 'unimportant soldiers' would pay the price.' Gabby's eyes glimmered in victory, as several more people joined in the murmuring. She smiled, smoothing her Mohawk down to one side, a habit she had grown used to whilst in the council guards' ranks.

'If you would let me finish Gabby,' Sheeva's usual serene voice rang out with authority across the room. Gabby rolled her eyes and sat again, twisting the piercing in her eyebrow as she did, her passive aggressive way of showing she would be quiet but had no intention of listening.

'I was about to say that the reason Thomas is more important is because of what he is. As a changeling wizard, he will need to maintain his illusion to keep his identity safe and I'm willing to bet that Eli has figured out by now that if he takes that power it will only be a matter of time before they can use magic to get inside his head. Even Thomas has his limits.' Stunned silence met her.

Eyes moved back and forth between Sheeva and Gabby, who was on her feet again.

'Once again. Thomas knew the risks. I've known him for longer than most of you here and I believe he would not want us to even contemplate a rescue,' Gabby looked incredulous.

'I agree,' Sheeva said quietly. For once Gabby was at a loss for words. 'Thomas would not want us to risk ourselves ordinarily but what you must understand is that Thomas alone knows the location and identities of all of the resistance members. His gift for illusion went beyond that of an ordinary changeling. He could retain and recall more information than any other magical being I have ever known. The truth is if Eli gets into Thomas' mind, we won't lose one or two of our soldiers, we're all lost.' Silence prevailed. Gabby sat down picking at her piercings, momentarily subdued by this revelation. 'If we are to survive this, we have to rescue Thomas, it's our only hope,' Sheeva informed the now panicked assembly.

'Then we disband the resistance; we run. Regina is lost anyway, she was the key, without her we have no proof of Eli's corruption. I say we run and live to fight another day,' Gabby's eyes met Sheeva's, defiance sparked there. Sheeva regarded the rebellious Vampire, frustration threatening to spill from her lips in a scream.

'Are you actually THAT stupid?' Heads whipped towards Martha, who was now stood, face set in determination. A few witches and Vampires actually moved back as if they fully expected Gabby and Martha to come to blows. Gabby was stunned for second but not for long, she regained her cool as quickly as she had lost it.

'What did you say to me?' Gabby growled.

'You heard me, you selfish, stupid blood sucker,' Martha's wand appeared in her hand and those gathered moved back. John grabbed a vase from the table moving it to safety before returning to his armchair by the fire, his lids beginning to droop already.

'My family have died for this resistance...died. How many here have lost their loved ones to this fight?' She looked around the room. Saddened eyes met hers, fresh pain plainly there to see. 'I don't know about you Gabby, but I've seen enough death. You really think you can run away from this? Once Eli has our names there won't be a hole deep enough to hide in. He will hunt us all down. We ...' Martha gestured around the room, 'might as well just walk into the Council of Elders' chambers and confess right now.'

'You can't ask people to die for your monster of a niece, or for some wrinkled old leader who was naïve enough to believe that Eli Masters had an ounce of compassion left in that black heart of his,' Gabby spat out, her eyes flashing dangerously. Complete silence met her outburst.

'No-one is forcing anyone to do anything,' Martha growled, the knuckles wrapped around her wand turned white in anger.

'Martha's right,' Sheeva interjected, 'If any of you gathered here this evening feel you would like to leave, go ahead. I intend to fight, I intend to rescue Thomas, I intend to ensure the future of all our people by removing Eli from power. If that costs me my life, so be it.' For a moment no-one spoke. Then slowly, one by one vampires, wolves, witches, wizards, trolls all raised their voices in support and were on their feet, all eyes on Sheeva with renewed respect. Gabby bristled and shifted uncomfortably. All fight appeared vanquished in the vampire, who liked nothing better than to create chaos wherever she went. It was that mischievous, rebellious side, which had drawn her to the resistance initially and made her such a valuable asset.

'Well Gabby, it appears you're alone in your concerns. Feel free to take your leave, if that is your desire,' Sheeva fought a smirk, she knew that now there was no chance of an uprising, the young vampire would back down.

'I never said I wouldn't fight, I was just pointing out that others might object. That's all,' she grumped as she sat back down; daring someone to try and kick her out, glaring pointedly at Martha.

'That's settled then,' Sheeva declared. 'As soon as we are able, we will rescue Thomas.'

'What about Regina?' Martha ventured but there was an echo of hopelessness in her voice, 'Is there any hope for her?'

'Martha,' Sheeva's eyes met hers as she spoke, 'You have lost much more than any of us could ever imagine. I do not know if escape from the darkness is possible but I promise you this, if there is any chance at all, even a speck, I will do anything and everything to bring her home to you.' She patted Martha's shoulder tenderly before being pulled into an embrace, her eyes filled with tears as the homely woman murmured thank yous.

'So what now?' Gabby asked a bored note in her voice.

'Now, we go to war,' Sheeva declared.

Chapter 11

The way through

Since the beginning of all that is, a passage led the way from the land of the living to the other place. But the hate of the other place seeped into the passage and severed the path, blocking the way through.

That evening was one of the best Regina had had in a long time despite being trapped in the darkness, facing unknown odds with no idea if they could even break through and get home again. It had been so long since she'd felt happy, that it almost felt alien to her. She resisted the urge to hunt that night, only because her father hadn't let her out of his sight for a second. Instead she swallowed her pride and asked Imogen for a little of her blood, under the condition that she drink some herself. She had relented and the change was almost instantaneous, colour flew to Imogen's cheeks; her cheekbones slightly less sharp.

As they set out into the purple lit wild, Regina shoved the remaining blood into the bag, all the while ignoring her monster's protestations, that the blood from the hunt was superior. As Regina crumbled some biscuits into a grateful Gerald's pot, Regina's hands grazed something cold and hard in the bag and pulled it out. It was the bracelet Poppy had given her the very first time they met. Regina slipped it over her hand and shimmied it onto her wrist, admiring the delicate moon and sun.

D M Singh

'This is it,' Baby declared as they reached the seam. Aurora scuttled away from it, looking nervous. Up close it was beautiful, a glimmer of hope and light in this endless dark. Regina knew now, why the souls were drawn to it.

'So how do we do this?' Regina asked.

'How did you get here?' Baby asked. Regina remembered the spell, she pulled the athame from the bag and mumbled an apology to the now grumbling Gerald, who had been napping happily.

'Ready?' She asked. Aurora shook her head frantically but they paid her no mind. She was known for her cruelty but not her bravery. Slowly Regina dragged the blade across her palm, wincing as she did. Her monster was right, the blood from the bag did not satiate her enough; she would not heal quickly. She felt weak. Grasping the athame, she drew the blood down the seam whispering the words over and over again, '*Ostium Interim.*' Nothing. At least I didn't burst into flames she thought to herself.

'Why isn't it working?' Imogen wondered.

'What were you thinking about the last time Regina? Try, remember and concentrate on that,' Poppy suggested. Regina nodded and repeated the process, this time she let herself think of him. His eyes, his smile, his laugh …

'It's working,' Aurora screamed clapping excitedly.

'Luckily for you,' Regina scowled back at her, 'I'll go alone, just in case.' Emile started to protest, but Baby set him straight.

'It has to be this way Emile. She is the one who opened the way through, she must be the first. She will be safe,' she assured him. 'We won't be far behind.' Regina saw the pain in her father's eyes, she knew he could not bear to be parted after all that had happened, but this was their chance.

'I'll be fine. Give it one minute then follow,' Regina

instructed. Imogen nodded. The seam was warm and enveloped her in flash of light, then the dark returned. She stepped through pushing her way to the Other Place, taking a shaky breath as she did. She had expected it to be as different as night and day, literally. The darkness was all encompassing as she emerged. Heavier than even the Darkness.

This was not the place of myth, the place she had read about, that place was like heaven from what she could make out and this felt like it was hell. Screeches and screams filled the air and as Regina's light orb bobbed ahead. Red eyes glinted in the dark. Regina screamed and ran, not knowing where she would go. The darkness was thicker here, filling every corner. Regina's breath came in great rattling gasps as she ran. Her light orb was rendered useless as it struggled to keep up with her. Her foot connected with something and before she could stop herself she was on the floor. Her head snapped up instinctively, checking for the eyes that had sent her dashing into the unknown. Nothing! Where was it? The light orb had finally caught up and as Regina looked down, she saw her foot was twisted the wrong way and her stomach lurched. It didn't hurt, thanks to the blood she had consumed not long ago but it wasn't healing. She dragged herself to her knees scanning for the creature she had seen, still nothing. All she could do was wait for the others, they wouldn't be far behind her. Regina winced as she gingerly manoeuvred herself into a seated position. Her head ached and before she could call out in pain, there was a flash of light and she was out.

'She couldn't have gone further than this?' Aurora complained for the millionth time since making their way through the seam, 'can't we stop for a minute? We've been walking for ages.' Imogen growled at her and she stuck her tongue out like a petulant child.

'We need to keep moving until we find shelter, we have

no idea what may await us in this place,' Baby shuddered.

'I don't understand,' Imogen shouted coming to a stop, 'this is the Other Place right? So shouldn't it be ... I don't know, a little bit nicer?' She threw her hands up in frustration.

'The magic one was delighted, all those in the Other Place were now filled with all the rage and heartache he was, because their loved ones could never come through the passage. Those who died, and tried to pass through were trapped in eternal darkness, neither in this place or that, most driven mad with nothing but memories and regrets for company. The day came however that the blood spiller who had loved the magic one so passionately, discovered a way to die and believed that she would at last be with her love. But the damage was done, the bitterness of the magic one had ruined any chance of their reunion and the blood spiller was trapped forever in darkness driven mad by the love she had lost.' Poppy rattled the story off verbatim, a far-away look in her eyes.

'You've been here though Poppy, for your soul sitting?' Imogen asked. Poppy nodded. 'Was it like this then?'

Poppy shook her head, 'it was ... somewhat darker than I had expected but it was nowhere near this bad. It feels different, darker. I can't describe it, it feels ...'

'Wrong?' Dragmir supplied. She nodded.

'We need to keep looking for Reggie. If she's out here anything could have happened to her. You saw those things when we came through,' Emile pleaded, desperate to have his daughter safe and in his arms again.

'We need to be practical,' Baby insisted, 'we can't just run around in circles trying to find her. She will try and find Helena and Jay, so we'll do the same. We will find her.' She assured Emile, who said nothing but nodded as he raked his hands through his hair in frustration.

'So how do we find Helena?' Poppy asked Baby, who looked just as lost as the others.

'We go to the source of all of this ...' Dragmir gestured, 'we find Alexander.'

Baby blanched at the name.

'He is the magic one who started this?' She asked, a look of sadness in her huge eyes.

'Yes. He caused all of this, during my time in the darkness I researched the myth and found him to be the most likely culprit.' He shot Baby an apologetic look. Baby shook, her large body shifting and phasing. It was unsettling and Imogen had a feeling it was due to lack of control. Black smoke swirled, encircling Baby. The howling wind surrounding them deafening in this otherwise silent place. Above the din, Baby's cry of *'Not now Davina'* could be heard. The winds died and the smoke changed its hue, as crimson replaced the black. When all was quiet again Davina stood, a murderous look on her face.

'You knew Dragmir, you knew all this time it was him!' She accused, her eyes flashed red and Poppy took a cautionary step away from Dragmir.

'I am sorry I deceived you Davina, but what purpose would it have served for you to know. I knew you would drive yourself crazy trying to get to him,' Dragmir stood his ground. Imogen had noticed that he did not flinch as the others did when confronted by Davina and she wondered if he was powerful enough not to fear her or simply stupid enough to believe she wouldn't crush him. Davina's eyes never left Dragmir, circling him as he spoke, like a hunter assessing its prey.

'You had no right to keep it from me,' she screeched, eyes ablaze with rage, 'you were my only friend in this place and you lied.' She leapt before anyone could react, not that they could have stopped her. She still retained her magic and abilities, whilst the others grew weaker, hour by hour.

Dragmir blocked her fireball but did not move quick enough to escape her talons and teeth. She shredded his chest with her talons, her eyes gleaming with delight as blood seeped from his wounds, dripping onto the ground. He had no time to recover, her teeth were at his throat, ripping and draining. Dragmir cried out but stood his ground. Suddenly she was thrown clear, her head slamming into a nearby tree. Imogen looked around at the others to see who could have done it. They looked just as bewildered as she.

'Stop Davina!' Baby screamed. Davina looked shocked that Baby's words had spilled from her lips.

'How?' Davina asked examining herself, as though to double check she hadn't become a dragon. She shook her head and launched herself at Dragmir only to be thrown back again, this time her head hit the trunk of the dead tree with a sickening crunch. Dragmir approached her, examining her head.

'She'll be fine but we'll have to carry her,' and with that he swung her over his shoulder and continued on.

'Hold up,' Imogen shouted, running to keep up, 'what just happened? And who the hell is Alexander?'

Dragmir hoisted Davina further up his shoulder, not missing a stride as he did and Imogen wondered once more, how powerful he was. He appeared completely unharmed by Davina's attack and as they walked on, she noted he did not tire as they did.

'We have to keep moving. I am more than happy to tell you, if you can keep up,' he mocked. Imogen growled at him lengthening her stride to match his.

'Talk,' she commanded. Aurora, Poppy and Emile had joined them, no doubt eager for an explanation too.

'You all know the myth,' he stated.

'We must have read that thing a hundred times since we got here,' Aurora whined. Imogen gave her a look that promised pain if she didn't stop her lips flapping, Aurora growled but fell silent.

'The magic one is Alexander, an ancient and powerful wizard. Like the story says his true love was a vampire who was so desperate to follow him, she followed him into the Darkness. She planned to pass through to the Other Place. However it was not permitted, she was cast out and though she tried and tried she could not find a way to join him. That vampire was Davina.' Dragmir rubbed his hands along his jawline, scrubbing his fingers through his beard; lost in thought.

'So the man she loved, drove her mad?' Poppy asked. 'How horrible.'

'Now you see why I didn't tell her sooner. Davina would have burnt The Darkness to the ground had I told her. You may have noticed, she has a bit of a temper,' Dragmir added.

'Didn't you think we should have known this?' Emile demanded, 'who knows what we're walking into? Or what Davina might do once she awakens. You put us all in danger with your selfishness. You put her in danger,' he seethed.

'I may not know Regina as well as you but I know her well enough to know that she would dive head first into any danger to rescue her friend, to rescue any of you. I have an idea of how we can find Alexander and right now he is our only lead and hope to get out of here. So that's where I'm going, you can belly-ache about being excluded, or you can join me and hope that Regina is there waiting.' His eyes flashed and Imogen flinched, there was a darkness in him she hadn't seen before, it grinned behind his eyes. No one spoke but followed the ancient vampire as he led the way towards Alexander and away from the red eyes that glimmered in the darkness behind them.

D M Singh

Chapter 12

Fern

Lithiana was betrayed. Her aura sparked as she flung the door of Poppy's elf dwelling open. For over a thousand years she had lived in these forests, led these people, she had always known what was best for them. As an immortal she understood the big picture. In the grand scheme of things, the life of one filthy, hybrid child meant nothing. And so when Helena had come to her, telling Lithiana she knew where the hybrid was, that she could turn Regina and use her for their benefit, Lithiana had done something she had done only once before in her extremely long life; trusted.

Now as she angrily picked through the dusty remains of Poppy's life, she cursed her own naivety. Helena had played on her weakness, she saw that now. Lithiana longed to go back to the days when elves were respected by humans, the days when elves had lived free, no skulking behind illusions and spells, no need to hide their tell-tale features when mixing with mortals.

She scoured through what remained of Poppy's things. They stood in tall chests, bulging at their tattered seams. Lithiana flicked open the catch of the nearest one. Inside, jars of ingredients for healing lay upon the silken inners. She knew Poppy had what she was looking for, Poppy's mother had shown it to Lithiana decades ago. It contained the kind of magic that could destroy or give life, depending on the person who harnessed its power. Magic was usually dark or light but this particular item contained both, it was the last of its kind. Lithiana knew her involvement with Helena could be discovered at any time and something like the bracelet could be the answer.

The door creaked open and Lithiana slammed the trunk shut quickly. Fern shuffled through the door, humming as she did.

'Lithiana? I didn't expect to see you here,' Fern said looking confused. Lithiana never wandered down this far into the village. She was always so busy, either bustling between meetings across the market square or else attending the Council of Elder's meetings in London.

'I was feeling … nostalgic,' Lithiana shrugged, opening a trunk and fingering through a few photographs.

'Well don't mind me Lithiana, I've just come to clear the last of Poppy's things. She will be nymph now. I'll store her things until she claims them again.' Fern set about her task, pulling a pouch of lilac coloured powder out of her pocket, which she sprinkled on four of the trunks. The trunks immediately emitted a high pitched squeal, before shrinking to the size of a matchbox. Fern continued her humming as she stooped to retrieve the trunks and placed them in her satchel.

'You knew Poppy well, did you not Fern?' Lithiana asked changing tack, she might never find what she wanted by scrambling around looking for it. The bracelet was imbibed with such protection that magic would be unable to find it. Perhaps Poppy had entrusted it to someone. After all it would have been foolish of her to leave something so powerful lying around for anyone to claim.

'Yes. I knew her mother before she passed, Poppy was like a daughter to me,' she said sadly. Though she knew Poppy was nymph by now and not gone forever, it meant she would not be permitted to live amongst the elves again, the thought filled Fern's heart with sorrow.

'Did she ever mention a bracelet? It was nothing, a trinket really, but since I was the one who gave it to her, I thought she wouldn't object if I took it back.'

'You know the law Lithiana,' Fern said looking surprised, 'those who move on must bequeath their possessions, the rest they must claim. You cannot claim that which is not yours Lithiana,' her eyes challenged Lithiana's. For a second Lithiana's aura pulsed, then calmed.

'Of course. I just wanted to see it one more time. It was my mother's you see, but you are right the law is the law,' she sighed and headed for the door.

'Wait,' Fern called as Lithiana turned the handle, 'I guess there's no harm in looking. What did it look like?'

'Silver with a moon and a star,' Lithiana said happily. Fern who had begun to search through the remaining trunks halted. She had seen that bracelet, only it wasn't Poppy's any longer. The last time she had seen her son, Regina had shoved it into her back pocket. From what Jay told her, it was an old trinket, but it had never belonged to Lithiana. Why the lie?

'Well if it's here I'm sure we'll find it,' she said cheerfully resuming her search.

Fern flicked her wrist and the fire roared to life in the hearth. She paced. The rug beneath her had been suffering ever since she had sent the message. Had it been five hours? What was taking them so long?

'Fern,' a voice hissed though the door.

'Who is it?' She whispered back.

'Sheeva sent me,' an impatient voice continued, 'let me in before I'm spotted.' Fern slid back the bolt and turned the lock. She was pushed back into her home, by a cloaked figure. Once inside, the mysterious stranger removed her hood and Fern found herself face to face with a mohawked vampire.

'I'm Gabby,' she said quickly, removing her cloak and revealing a snake tattoo which ran from her wrist to her shoulder.

'I'm sorry I asked you to come but I was afraid of who might intercept my message,' Fern said nervously. 'Tea?' She offered, grabbing a teapot which resembled a gingerbread house. Gabby shook her head and took Fern's place, pacing by the fire.

'I'd rather get down to business and get out of here if you don't mind,' Gabby picking at her lip ring as she spoke.

'Of course,' Fern apologised, 'the resistance suspected that someone in our community was working with Helena and I think I know who it is.' She bit her lip worriedly. Gabby stayed silent. 'Lithiana was poking through Poppy's things today. She claimed to have given something to Poppy but I know for a fact that the bracelet she was searching for never belonged to her. The magic contained in it is … dangerous.'

'How dangerous is dangerous?' Gabby enquired, scared that she already knew the answer.

'Dangerous enough to make contact with the resistance even though we're all being watched. If this bracelet falls into the wrong hands it could be catastrophic.' Fern raised the cup to her lips before placing it on the small coffee table. 'If I am right, then the most powerful elf I've ever known is the reason Poppy is dead, why all those at the resistance headquarters died. I can't believe she could be so … cold. But as long as Regina has the bracelet, we are safe.' Gabby shifted uncomfortable at the mention of Regina. The resistance had not yet told all its members about Helena taking Jay into The Darkness.

Gabby felt uneasy as she watched the homely elf sip her tea, oblivious to the fact that her son was missing, most likely dead and Regina along with him. She was suddenly glad she had listened to Sheeva and allowed Martha to enchant her necklace. It would keep her thoughts hidden and temporarily block Fern's ability to decipher truth from lies. 'So, what happens next?' Fern asked refilling her cup.

'Nothing,' Gabby said flatly. 'You will maintain your cover, observe Lithiana and report anything suspicious. She may still be in contact with those in league with Helena, if so, she could help lead us to them,' she nodded curtly and headed towards the door, eager to be gone.

'My son, how is he? I've not heard from him in a while. Is he well? Is Regina well?' Fern had abandoned her tea altogether, her eager eyes on Gabby's back.

'He is well, as is Regina. It is difficult to get messages out at the moment,' Gabby barked, she didn't mean to be harsh, but she could not afford to let this information out. The resistance had been on lock down ever since Regina had entered The Darkness. Sheeva had been clear that Fern could not know her son was gone. She was their only eyes in the elf village and they couldn't afford to lose her. As much as she hated to admit it, Gabby knew Sheeva was right. If Fern knew, she could abandon her assignment in search of a way to save to her son and who could blame her?

'Of course. All hands on deck, I know how close he and Regina became, I knew he'd be in the thick of it,' she smiled proudly and Gabby's silent heart ached for her.

'I'm sure he'll contact you, just as soon as it is safe,' she assured, her hand on the elf's shoulder. She smiled warmly, before replacing the hood of her cloak, stepping outside the elf dwelling and taking to the skies.

D M Singh

Chapter 13

The Magic One

The world shifted in and out of focus, lines blurred and sharpened, lights flashed and Regina clutched her head. Standing, she conjured a light orb, the room she was in was empty, cold and dank. There was a distinct coppery smell that Regina recognised as blood, it was freshly spilt. She swallowed hard, resisting the urge to find its source and take it for herself. She needed to find a way out of here, the others would be looking for her and she had no idea what was out there or what it could do to them. Outside the room she heard shuffling and scraping.

'Hello!' She called out, 'who's there?' As she moved towards the source of the noise she realised her hands were bound, she pulled at the seemingly weak bindings only to find they wouldn't shift. Her strength was failing her again, she needed blood. Her stomach rolled as she remembered the taste of The Lost soul's blood.

'Briseadh,' Regina commanded and her restraints fell to the floor. She ran to the wall running her hands along the rough stone, feeling for a way out. As her fingers skimmed the surface, she stopped suddenly, the scent of blood was stronger here. Perhaps whoever she heard was injured and on the other side of this wall. The hunger kicked in, as the monster inside took over. One kick and the stone caved in like paper. Regina's eyes searched through the rising dust and rubble. Slumped over at the bottom of a set of stone steps lay a figure dressed in ragged clothes, stained with blood. The smell made Regina's stomach turn. Whoever this was had been here a long time. Regina covered her mouth and nose.

'Are you okay?' She asked trying not to breathe in the over-whelming scent of rotting flesh and blood. The figure lunged for her suddenly, fangs bared and eyes wild.

'BACK YOU FILTHY CREATURE!' Light spilled down the steps, a deep, booming voice following. The creature hissed and scuttled into the corner, murmuring all the while. 'Well? Are you coming up Regina or do you wish to remain down there in the filth?' He turned and walked away, leaving the door open and Regina wondering who her rescuer was and how he knew her name.

A large, warm and well-lit room greeted Regina after her cautious ascent. She hastily shut the door behind her, ignoring the growling from below. If she didn't know better, she would have thought she was back in the mortal world. A large fire burned away in the cast iron grate. Above, hovered frames with moving pictures, a beautiful red-head laughing and smiling. Regina would recognise that face anywhere, she was looking at a much happier Davina. She screwed her eyes up as she examined each one. A large gilded frame bobbed just above Regina's head. The picture, almost brown in colour, housed a couple, who were gazing at each other as if they hadn't noticed the photographer.

'You have met my love I presume?' Regina jumped. Her rescuer or kidnapper, whoever he was had entered the room again without her realising, which was no mean feat.

'You knew Davina?' She asked carefully. He handed her a glass and seeing it was blood she accepted it gratefully and drank deeply.

'Oh yes. I have known her a very long time. She is my wife.' He lifted a glass of amber liquid to his lips. 'Unfortunately we have been apart since my death.' He sighed looking at the picture of the smiling red-haired beauty, loss in his eyes.

'But she's here,' Regina said. A glint of hope sparked

in his eyes.

'Really? I never thought … after everything I've done … I had hoped …can it be true?' He muttered to himself. He turned his piercing blue eyes on Regina. 'How is she here?'

'I came through the seam, she was with me. Well, she was going to follow but then it all went black. The next thing I knew, I was here.' She arched her brow. 'How did I get here?'

'Sorry about that. That was Druscilla I'm Afraid,' he said as if that explained it all. Regina just stared, waiting.

'Who is Druscilla?' She asked when he didn't volunteer any more information.

'Of course, you're new here. You met her briefly downstairs, she's a blood demon.'

'What the hell is a blood demon?' Regina wondered, hoping this was the last unknown nasty she would come across in this place.

'The vampires in this realm, the Other Place, have … evolved. When their loved ones could no longer pass through, they gave themselves completely to their baser instincts and began to feed on one another. It has driven them quite mad and as you saw from your brief time with Dru, they do not play well with others.'

'Why do you have one in your basement? Isn't she dangerous?' Regina glanced toward the door.

'She is no threat to me. They feed on other vampires, so I'm safe. I took Dru in years ago, before she became that … thing. She was weaker than the others, they terrorised her, fed on her over and over until she was almost drained. She is safe here, the others can't get past the warding's.' He gestured towards the window, where triskelle symbols were painted in what looked like blood and gold flecks. 'She escapes now and again. I feed her the best I can but she sometimes roams in search of a fresh kill. I must admit I'm surprised she brought you here and didn't kill you.'

His eyes searched Regina's, she quickly looked away. She didn't know if she could trust him. She wouldn't let him see what she was. Regina shrugged.

'I must not taste very good,' she laughed dryly. 'Hey, how did you know my name by the way?'

'Wizard,' he said simply as if that was enough of an explanation. 'I have a particular knack when it comes to reading people. You however, are a bit of a quandary my friend. Only managed to get your name.'

'Just weird that way I guess. Anyway, it's rude to poke around in other people's head. Didn't your mother ever tell you?' Regina shot him a tentative look. 'You know my name so it's only fair you tell me yours.'

'Alexander. Pleased to meet you Miss Regina,' he bowed, another indication he was from a different era. Regina fiddled with her bracelet, wondering where the others were and if they too had fallen victim to the red eyed demons.

'That's a lovely little trinket. May I?' Alexander looked eagerly at Regina's wrist. She extended her arm for him to get a better but did not remove it. As he did Regina noted that the moon was now luminous and the sun faded into the silvery background. 'Interesting,' he mused.

'What's interesting?' She asked. Curious herself to know what it meant. She had seen the change and was scared to ask Poppy about it. They had enough to worry about already.

'Well for one thing, I have heard of but never seen a Teljesitmeny before. Of course you know how to wield it?' His look said he doubted it.

'Of course I know how to wield it,' she prickled, 'but, I was curious, as to why the moon has changed?' She smoothed her finger over the moon as she spoke.

'Well,' Alexander started pompously, 'as an experienced Teljesitmeny bearer, you will have already realised that it feeds on your light or darker side?' He shot her a smug look as if he knew she had no clue what she had around her wrist. 'If it is kept in balance it acts as a powerful protection to the wearer.' Regina nodded. She knew it offered protection, Imogen had hinted as much but things had happened so fast after that, she hadn't had time to ask her or Poppy anymore about it. 'However, if the wearer strays too far to the darker side, it becomes less of a protector and more of an extension of that darkness.'

Regina dropped all pretences at this news, 'what do you mean?'

'The darkness infects the magic. It influences the wearer's decisions and forces their hand if necessary. Once you have chosen the darkness completely, the Teljesitmeny craves it, so in order to feed itself...'

'I literally go over to the dark side,' Regina finished. She grabbed the clasp and yanked, but it would not budge, even using all of her vampire strength. As she moved her hand from the clasp to think which spell she might use to move it, the delicate links from the bracelet stabbed into her wrist and wound its way under her skin, snaking its way up her forearm. Regina fell to the floor, clutching her arm as she did.

'Looks like you've chosen,' Alexander said, not moving to help as the bracelet pushed its way up through her forearm and toward her shoulder. Finally it stopped and Regina knelt on the floor, taking great shuddering breaths, tears rolled down her face. Her wrist healed around the wound where the Teljesitmeny had invaded her body. She shakily got to her feet, examining her arm as she did. Beneath the skin the links were visible. They flexed and shimmered just under the surface.

'GET IT OUT!' She screamed as another jolt of pain racked through her body. Alexander simply shook his head.

'I'm afraid it is beyond my magic. Once it has a hold on its host, it is down to you. The decisions you make from now on will determine whether it takes over you, or falls away.' He examined her arm with a strange look of fascination in his eyes.

'Forget magic, rip it out,' she rummaged in her bag and retrieved her athame and handed it to him.

'I don't think that's a good idea,' he backed up handing it back to a frustrated Regina. From inside her bag, Gerald was voicing his opinion very loudly, as scolding squeaks and shouts reached her ears.

'Sorry fella,' she whispered as she closed the bag to his protestations. 'I'll do it myself,' she growled and then winced as the links climbed higher. She hacked at the bracelet first, nothing. She would have to cut it out. She bit her lip and sliced through her wrist and followed the links up pulling it as she went. Blood dripped down her arm and it took everything for her not to stop, to not give in to the pain and pass out. She knew she had to get it out, with her monster teetering so close to the surface these days, she was prone to dark outbursts. She would not give her power up to yet another monster. Before she could pull it free, barbs burst forth from the links, slithered their way back under her flesh and wrapped themselves tighter.

'Stop it,' Alexander begged, pulling the athame from her hand and throwing it to the ground, 'it's killing you,' his eyes pleaded. Regina's arm, now drenched in blood began to turn a shade of blue, as if the links were a boa constrictor squeezing the life out of her. The moment she stopped struggling, the barbs, though now latched onto her flesh released their stranglehold on her. 'I know you want that thing out, but this isn't working. Maybe we can find someone who knows how this thing works?' Regina wasn't happy that he was right, she could feel the darkness seeping into her very blood. She had to find the others, she had to see Poppy. She'd know what to do.

Chapter 14

Secrets

The alarms screeched out a cry of protest in the darkness and Eli masters was on his feet immediately; wand trained on the door of his office. It burst open admitting his assistant, his yellowed werewolf eyes glimmering through the darkness.

'Is it them?' Eli demanded. The werewolf gave a jerky nod of his head before turning and tearing down the corridor towards the sound of the disturbance. Wand still in hand, Eli ran his hand along the wood of the oak fireplace till his finger found the switch. He flicked it and after a quick glance behind him, climbed through to the passage behind the chimney and coals, the small door swinging closed behind him taking with it the screams of the resistance and his Death Squad.

The main meeting hall at the Council of Elder's chambers was truly beautiful. The green marbled floor formed a spiral that swept out toward the twelve thrones that lined the circular room. Above each of the thrones, a carving of the species represented. Witch, vampire, unicorn, werewolf, dwarf, elf, nymph, troll, ogre, giant, omen bringers and finally one for the head of the council of elders. Sheeva had always thought this room sacred, she had felt most at peace in this room. That illusion was forever shattered as spells and curses flew from wands, bodies crumpled and blood flowed across the tiled floor.

A werewolf howled a call to arms before it was brought down by Gabby, she spun and sliced through the Death

Squad, a deadly but graceful dance. Martha screamed curses under her breath, sending a vampire hurtling through the air and landing with a sickening crunch on the opposite side of the room. Sheeva flickered between her tiny form and normal size, shrinking to avoid spells; the bow she carried firing spelled arrows. Sheeva slipped as she leapt over a lunging werewolf, she hit the floor hard, the breath knocked from her body. Before she had time to react, the werewolf was on her, but it whimpered and collapsed on top of her, blood filling its eyes and dripping from its mouth. Strong hands lifted the wolf off and a bloody hand helped her to her feet. Sheeva came face to face with her unlikely saviour, John, Martha's sleepy husband, grinned at her before dashing after a vampire.

'GET TO THOMAS, WE'LL HOLD THEM OFF AS LONG AS WE CAN,' he cried over his shoulder. Sheeva nodded, looking for a way out. Death squad members fell all around, but so too did members of the resistance.

'THIS WAY,' Gabby called. Sheeva flickered, changed and flew through the gap Gabby had created. Changing was risky, she was a smaller target like this, true, but she was weaker.

Eli's office was empty, Sheeva had expected as much. He was never one to fight his own battles. She shimmered back to her full size. She knew every inch of this place. She'd scoured the blueprints and knew there was a secret passage in here; she just needed to find it. Sheeva didn't believe for one minute that Eli had left the council chambers, not when he was so close to breaking Thomas. She searched the bookcases and sconces for a lever or switch.

'Traitor!' A voice growled from the doorway. Sheeva grabbed her bow and fired but the werewolf was too quick, dodging the deadly projectiles easily.

'Julian, is that you?' Sheeva smirked, 'Eli's abandoned you, turned tail and run like the coward he is. He didn't even stop to grab the 'oh –so-important resistance leader,' she taunted.

'He would never abandon me. You really think he would leave Thomas behind for you turncoats?' Julian had shifted back now and was circling Sheeva, his yellow wolf eyes still firmly fixed on his prey.

'Well I don't see him,' Sheeva countered, 'I always knew he was a coward but I had no idea he was this cowardly.' Julian sneered, his lip curled back and a low growl rumbled from his chest.

'It's all part of the plan,' he snapped.

'Plan?' Sheeva asked sounding intrigued.

'Nice try,' Julian snarled.

'Oh …I understand Eli didn't tell you the plan, I always thought he told you everything. My mistake,' she shrugged. Julian prickled at this.

'I know that while you're wasting your time chatting with me. Eli has already made it down to the lower levels. It'll all be over soon enough Sheeva,' Julian's eyes darted toward the fireplace and back again quickly, 'Thomas will spill his secrets and …' Julian's bragging was interrupted by a swift roundhouse kick to face followed by a well-aimed spell which knocked him flat on his back, he fell to the ground, a look of shock on his face. Sheeva stood over him grinning.

'You never could keep your mouth shut Julian. Thanks, I'll make sure Eli knows how helpful you were.' She opened her palm and a translucent powder hovered, swirling above him. Julian coughed as the substance filtered into his lungs and he went limp. Sheeva ran to the fireplace, feeling beneath the mantle for a switch. A clunk sounded and Sheeva smiled to herself before transforming and flying into the darkened passageway.

The sounds of the battle above had long since faded. Eli barked orders at the guards on the lower levels and they scurried towards the hidden staircase he had just descended. He knew if the resistance got through they wouldn't last long, but at least the guards' lives would buy him the time he needed. Thomas was on the brink of cracking. Once he had the names, the whole magical community could not fail to back him in his bid to exterminate the traitorous rats for good.

'Aperi,' he shouted. The door to Thomas' cell came clean off its hinges, slamming into the stone wall behind it. Darkness engulfed Eli, he could hear Thomas murmuring to himself as he entered, still under the enchantments Eli had placed on him. 'Lux,' he muttered into the dark. Immediately the torches which lined the walls flickered, before steadily glowing. Thomas sat in the middle of the room. Thanks to the enchantments, he needed no restraints, believing he was in a place with no escape. Eli had even spelled him to think he could no longer move. He waved his wand and lifted the visual illusion Thomas had been trapped in. Thomas gasped and blinked his eyes, the sudden light like daggers to his corneas. His arms remained at his side, as useless as his other powers. His blue eyes finally settled on Eli and a snarl that Regina would have been proud of, tore from his throat.

'It's time Thomas,' Eli sneered menacingly, 'time to give up your friends. I personally would have preferred to let you go slowly mad and take the information from you, however your little band of idiots have other plans and so there is no time for finesse, I'll just have to push you the rest of the way. Oh well, brute force it is,' he grinned maliciously.

'Depleo,' Eli whispered. Thomas' eyes widened, recognising the spell. Hot, searing pain clawed at his heart and up through his chest. Thomas coughed as blood spilled from his lips. He screamed a rattling, choked sound as blood gurgled in his throat. Tears of hot, crimson blood streaked down his face. He concentrated on his illusion. He had to hold on, just a little longer. His eyes rolled up, blood pouring from them now, he felt the pressure building in his head, slowly at first and then so intense Thomas felt for sure his illusion had slipped.

Down the hall, Sheeva had dispatched four of the Death Squad and was locked in combat with a particularly venomous vampire. He leapt into the air, blades aimed at Sheeva's throat. Sheeva dodged the attack. Spinning around before transforming and reappearing behind the vampire. The vampire's eyes bulged and he opened his mouth in surprise as Sheeva pulled his heart from his body. She whispered to the blackened lump and watched as it burst into flames turning to ash in her palm. He crumpled, just as Sheeva heard a scream. Was she too late?

'Thomas,' she whispered. She wiped the blood from her hands and sprinted in the direction of the cries.

'That's it, give in,' Eli grasped Thomas' shoulders, watching as the illusion finally started to fade. Wrinkles smoothed out, patchy hair grew brown and healthy in place of the thin, brittle hair Thomas had sported for over sixteen years. 'No, no It can't be you, you're dead, how …' Eli quickly backed away from Thomas, shaking his head in disbelief. He was so shocked by the discovery, he didn't hear Sheeva enter the room and by the time he realised it was too late. Before he could infiltrate his mind, Sheeva hit him with a powerful stunning spell that sent Eli clear across the room. Her eyes met Thomas' and for a second she said nothing, her mouth open in disbelief and then without another word she leaned in and slapped Thomas hard across the face.

D M Singh

Chapter 15

Jay

A wintery chill splintered through Jay's veins to his bones. The air fogged around him in the dark. He had lost track of time. The last thing he remembered, was fighting Helena at the house next to the loch. He remembered the look on Regina's face as Helena dragged him into The Darkness. He had no idea if Helena actually needed him for some nefarious plan or if she was simply cruel and enjoyed watching him suffer? He suspected a little of both. One thing he did know, Regina would try and find him. There had been loss in her eyes for a moment but it was quickly replaced with a determined spark that scared Jay. The Darkness filled him and he shivered; Regina wouldn't not do well in this place.

Whatever Helena had done to him when she pulled him through The Darkness, had made him more pliable and easy to control. He phased in and out of consciousness, unsure what was real. He had been dragged along from place to place, at one point he had imagined a ruby-red haired vampire and even thought he had seen a dragon.

He was somewhere different now, he was sure of that. The magic was suffocating in The Darkness and he had succumbed to every despondent thought. Every negative outcome drawing him deeper into hopelessness. Jay still felt remnants of despondency but it was no longer as strong and little hope slipped in. Whatever Helena had done to him seemed to be losing its hold. If he could just hold on a little longer, get a little stronger, perhaps he could escape. He had no idea if he could or what he would do once he managed to break free, but he had to try.

Outside the room he heard voices. It was Helena and a man he did not recognise. Jay crawled weakly toward the door to listen.

'How do you know Regina's the one?' He asked.

'You've met Alexander and Davina, so you know the story is not just a legend. This could be our chance to be together again,' Helena said smoothly.

'Even if she is, how do we know that she can be trusted? Remember what happened last time my love. I cannot face losing you again.' The man sounded desperate and Jay heard Helena making soothing noises. Who was this man that had Helena sounding so … un-Helena-like?

'I have ways to keep us all safe. I have missed you but I have missed her too. Don't you want us to be able to live like a family, just like we always wanted?' Jay balked, what did they want Regina to do and why would Helena say she had missed her? This made no sense, Jay blinked, trying to clear his fuzzy head. The voices grew fainter as the sound of retreating footsteps echoed from outside the door. He would rest, for now that was all he could do. Jay rubbed his hands together for warmth, wishing his magic worked here. As he tried his best to drift off to sleep, his thoughts turned to Regina, the way she fidgeted with her hair when she was deep in thought, how she bit her lip when she was worried and her smile. He hadn't seen much of her smile in the time they had known each other. She had seen so much pain and loss for one so young. Jay marveled that she could smile at all. He wondered if she was here and if she knew how he felt. He smiled to himself and as he did, his hands sparked. Laughing to himself, Jay reveled in the warmth the spark elicited. It died quickly but it lasted long enough to give him a little more hope. He was getting stronger. Jay thought of Regina and no sooner had he pictured her face; his magic sparked again. It appeared that in this place hope or love fueled his magic.

'I'll see you soon Reggie,' he grinned to himself, as he flexed his magical muscles in the dark of his prison … waiting for his chance.

D M Singh

Chapter 16

Defiance

Martha and John were a wonder to behold. This sleepy and homely, middle-aged couple danced and spun, firing curses and dodging enemies left and right. Gabby couldn't help but begrudgingly admire their skills and their connection. They worked in perfect harmony, one defending and one attacking. The tiles below were slippery with the blood of the fallen.

'We have to go,' Gabby called above the cries of the wounded.

'We're not leaving without Thomas and Sheeva,' Martha argued. She jumped behind Eli's throne as a dagger landed in the wood just inches from her face.

'She's been gone too long. We have to think about the others now. If they have the names we have to move the others before it's too late,' Gabby countered. Martha hesitated, wand raised deep in thought.

'You go, we'll wait,' she nodded toward her husband who was fighting a troll. She gave a weak smile before jumping from her hiding place swearing at the troll and shooting curses as she ran. Gabby threw the vial she was holding, a thick smoke engulfed her and then she was gone.

'I deserved that,' Thomas croaked as he tried to stand finally free of the spell. Sheeva was shaking. Tears streamed down her face, her eyes wild with anger. Before Sheeva stood Thomas, the real Thomas. He was taller, younger, dark brown hair now covered his head, wrinkles smoothed out apart from a few lines around the corners of his eyes and his mouth. His eyes remained the same, bold and strong.

'How could you?' She spat, wiping her tears angrily. Thomas knew nothing he said would ever be enough or ever make up for the pain he had caused her; his Sheeva.

'I know you want answers but we must go. I promise I will tell you everything,' Thomas soothed. His eyes met Sheeva's and she nodded mechanically, her eyes empty.

John dove behind a pillar which splintered into pieces from the curse a particularly skilled witch had flung at him. He landed and rolled with the vigour and agility of a man half his age and size.

'JOHN!' Martha screamed from the other side of the council chambers as a werewolf leapt towards her, knocking the wand from her hand. John was helpless, pinned down by the witch's curses flying all around him. Suddenly an explosion ripped through the room, members of the Death Squad and resistance were knocked from their feet; some flew across the room, slamming into walls. A blinding flash swept the room. John closed his eyes for fear it would burn the eyes from his head. When he opened them he was in the safe house, along with all the other members of the resistance. In the middle of the room stood Sheeva and another familiar looking figure. His eyes scoured the chaos for Martha. She was already on her feet, her eyes fixed on the figure in the middle of the room; her face drained of all colour. She stumbled through the bodies littered on the floor. Reaching out she touched his face before she erupted into laughter and fell into his arms.

'Brother,' she breathed. Eyes turned towards their leader in shock, as the realisation hit home that before them stood Thomas Bookden.

Curious members of the resistance had long since retired to the rooms upstairs. The dead had been buried in the back garden. Sheeva spelled a tree to grow there, one which could never be torn down or die. She remained stoic throughout it all. After the initial shock, the other members had accepted who Thomas really was easily, after all, he cut a more imposing figure now. Martha had followed him around everywhere hanging on his every word. John simply looked bemused. Several of the injured had been given make-shift beds in the living rooms and so Martha, John, Sheeva and Thomas made their way through to the study, after clearing away the potions they had used to heal the injured. Regina's mother, Evelyn, had been sent away to a safe place with trusted members of the resistance.

'I know you must all have questions,' Thomas said, as he closed the sliding doors behind them.

'You think?' Sheeva growled, her brow raised in challenge, anger dripping from every syllable. Martha's eye's darted between the two looking confused.

'I'm sorry. Am I missing something?' She asked taking a seat beside her husband, who for once was not asleep but watching the scene unfold, eyes wide.

'Yes Thomas, do tell Martha what she's missing. How we met, how we fell in love and how you disappeared when your family were murdered. I searched for you for years, I never gave up. I joined the resistance in the hope that one day I would find you and you were here all along. You made a fool of me,' Sheeva seethed, before stomping from the room.

'Oh my,' John piped up, 'you're in the dog house now Thomas.' Martha shot him a dangerous look, quieting his mirth.

'She's not the only one who deserves answers,' Martha declared, 'you left us long before any trouble with the

Death Squads and Eli. Where have you been? Why hide who you were?'

'I'm ashamed to admit that when Evelyn met Emile, I argued with our parents about them being together. I thought their union was … wrong. I warned it would only bring trouble. Father told me that he would not hear such bigotry spoken in his house, that he couldn't believe I could be so narrow-minded. I warned him that the council would hunt them if they ever had children but he believed that Eli would see reason. So I left. I was a coward.' He paused, as if expecting his sister to agree with his conclusion but she remained silent. Waiting. 'I travelled to Romania, took a job at a small school and tried to forget my family. While I was there I met an Elf, we fell in love. I knew I had to return but I was too late. I travelled to England alone, telling Sheeva I would return within the week. After arriving in London, I heard what had happened to our parents and had no idea what had become of you and your family. I was horrified to think what could have happened to Evelyn and Emile. After a night of feeling guilty and some heavy drinking, I realised I had a chance to help you, Evelyn and Emile. No one was looking for the cowardly brother. I realised if I kept myself hidden, I could find you and at least try to keep you all safe. So Thomas Bookden died and Thomas the leader of the resistance was born. Unfortunately it meant no-one could know my secret and so I never returned to Sheeva. Her life as an elf came to an end after entering a particularly nasty werewolf den, looking for me. She reappeared in her nymph form in London and I recruited her immediately.'

'Is that true?' Sheeva's voice was a whisper. Thomas had not heard her enter the room, her eyes reddened from her tears. He nodded.

'It killed me to leave you, I knew what it would do to you but I knew I had to try and save them. It was the least

I could do after abandoning them. If I had stayed, perhaps …' He stopped and shook his head.

'You couldn't have stopped Eli. Mum and dad knew what might happen to them but they loved Regina so much and so they couldn't comprehend that anyone would see her as a monster.' Martha had risen from the couch and laid her hand comfortingly on her younger brother's arm. Sheeva stood watching Thomas intently, an edge in her eyes that hadn't been there before. 'Come on John, let's check on the kids,' she said as she reached the door.

'They're fine, besides I just got all comfy,' he groaned. Martha shot a look that John recognised as one not to be argued with and immediately jumped to his feet, following her from the room.

'I'm so sorry,' Thomas closed the gap between them in an instant. His eyes searching her face. Sheeva's face was hard as he examined it but her lip trembled slightly, betraying her emotions. The ones she had kept in check and hidden for so long, just so she could function and move on. She had given up hope, because hope made her weak and got her killed.

'If there was a way I could have told you without putting everything and everyone in jeopardy, I would have,' his voice thick, as his eyes held hers captive. He reached across and stroked her cheek. That was her undoing, him touching her as she dreamed he would once more. Sheeva's breath hitched and she fell into his arms; her lips searching for his. All was forgotten in that moment, she had him back. Thomas; her Thomas.

Chapter 17

Alexander

'Where have you been?' Poppy snapped in a very un-nymph-like voice.

'To scout ahead,' Dragmir said quickly, 'I wanted to be sure the path was clear.'

'You've been gone for hours. What if she had woken?' Aurora barked, arms folded, looking thoroughly put out.

'I am sorry. You were all sleeping, I thought if I scouted ahead we could leave as soon as you awoke. I thought I was being followed but I was mistaken, I took the long way back to be safe,' Dragmir said apologetically.

'That was very thoughtful. Thankyou Dragmir,' Emile said, 'shall we proceed?' The others, however, looked mutinous.

They walked in uneasy silence with no light orbs to guide their way, they were at Dragmir's mercy. Dragmir surged ahead, Davina in his arms like she weighed nothing at all. Aurora followed eagerly, a suspicious Imogen at her side. Her eyes darting between Dragmir and Aurora, as if unable to decide whom she trusted the least.

'How can you trust him?' Poppy whispered to Emile. They'd lagged behind, just far enough not to be over-heard.

'I don't,' he hissed back. His eyes fixed on the vampire leading the way.

Poppy shot him a confused look, 'so why are you playing along?'

'I do believe one thing. He knows the way to Alexander and if he has Regina, that's all I care about.'

'Does Regina know?' Poppy asked, though she knew

the answer before she asked the question. Emile shook his head.

'She has enough to deal with. How has she been since?' His grief-filled eyes searched Poppy's.

'She's lost a lot,' Poppy said with a watery smile, 'she feels guilty. For you, for me, for Evelyn … for everyone. She has a good heart but sometimes I wonder how much more she can take.' Emile pondered this in silence and Poppy wondered if she should have sugar-coated it for him.

'This boy. Is he good enough for her?' He asked, his jaw set, looking every bit the murderous father you would fear meeting as a teenage boy.

'He is much like you Emile. He cares for her, anyone can see that. He makes her smile even through all of this. He gets through to her when no-one can. So yes I think he's good enough for Regina.' Emile stiffened, looking less than pleased. He grumped something about hormones and how he was at their age. Poppy laughed, 'see just like you,' she confirmed.

'I don't know if I can do it to her again Poppy. It's going to kill her, it's going to kill me,' he choked out the last words. Tears glistened in the eyes of this six foot, muscle-bound vampire and Poppy's heart ached for him.

'If I'm right about the legend then Regina has already changed things. There will be no more trapped loved ones in The Darkness. It may take time but eventually all will be as it was before. Friends and families re-united for eternity. I know it feels like forever and I know she is your little girl but she has changed, she is strong and one day you will have her with you forever. Right now, she needs us to remind her of who she is and what she's fighting for.' Poppy's eyes blazed determination. There would be time to feel sorry for themselves, but this was not the time. Emile met her gaze and nodded resolutely. They slipped back into silence. Poppy examined the vampire walking beside her and her heart broke a little for him. He had lost everything too.

Indigo hues hung above them as they approached a large castle. The grey stone of the walls and turrets blended into the fading light. It seemed night and day was easier to see in the Other Place.

'This is where Alexander lives?' Imogen asked, jogging to catch up with Dragmir.

'Yes,' he answered, lengthening his stride, 'best get there before nightfall,' he warned. Imogen glanced back, they were not alone.'

'Guys, pick up the pace,' Imogen called to Poppy and Emile. They glanced back and obliged. Poppy gasped realising they were approaching the castle and the drawbridge was not open; they would be trapped out here. 'A draw-bridge, an actual draw-bridge. A little ostentatious, don't you think?' Imogen shook her head as it lowered for them.

'Is he expecting us? …should we?' Poppy looked anxiously from the drawbridge to the approaching figures. They were wretched looking creatures that crawled like animals, but looked almost human; hissing and growling as they neared. A few stopped to attack others who'd wandered accidently into their path. Ripping the flesh from each other, chunks of flesh and skin and flying as they did.

'Draw-bridge it is,' Aurora called as she hurried across the draw-bridge. She flinched as she looked out into the endless dark abyss surrounding the castle.

'Nerves of steel that one,' Emile smirked before following her.

The ground shook beneath them as the drawbridge slammed closed. Just in time, as snarls and howls sounded from the other side. They stood in a grand courtyard, filled with flowers, grass cushioned their feet as they walked. In the very centre of the courtyard an immense fountain stood. A couple carved in stone gazed into each other's eyes, locked there in stony eternity. A red liquid shot both from the wand the man held and dripped from the woman's fangs. Imogen inhaled deeply, closing her eyes in happiness.

'Blood,' she cried, before racing over and scooping the velvety liquid into her parched mouth. She sighed contentedly and motioned for Emile to join her. Aurora ventured forth cautiously, approaching much like a lower ranking member of an animal pack. She watched Imogen to make sure she wouldn't shoo her away. Imogen growled but moved over so Aurora could quench her thirst.

'Is that Davina and Alexander?' Emile asked looking up at the fountain.

'Yes. He created this place for them. For the day they could finally be together again. Impressive is it not, what true love can do, even in the darkest of places.' Emile nodded, feeling a pang for his Evelyn, she had not returned to him since Regina had found him. One part of him was saddened another larger part hoped this meant she had woken in the mortal world and would be waiting for Regina when she returned. He whipped around, his eyes scouring the courtyard; that heartbeat. He knew that heartbeat.

'Dad?' Regina was leaning out of the window on the second floor. She smiled and stepped out and for a second Emile's breath caught. She flew through the air landing effortlessly on the floor before him. He scooped her into his arms and squeezed her as hard as he could, knowing he wouldn't be able to break her.

'How can you fly in this place?' He asked when he finally released her.

'I don't know. I find magic easier here than in The

Darkness. Now and then I get this surge of power, like some super-charged me. It's pretty cool,' she grinned excitedly.

'Are you … okay Reggie? You seem a little …' He broke off, not knowing what to say. Too happy, too cheerful, surely that's what he wanted for her.

'I'm fine dad. Quit worrying,' she teased before bouncing off, hugging an excited Poppy and even a very surprised Imogen.

'Alexander said you'd come. He explained everything. Come, meet him he's waiting.' And with that she leapt into the air, landing on the roof with a thud and disappeared through an open window.

The others exchanged a, *what the hell was that?* Look, before hurrying towards the large door which lay open.

D M Singh

Chapter 18

Strangers

The tree above the fallen bore fruit at an astounding rate. Their families had arrived after Thomas' liberation. All of them were relieved that the resistance's secrets were safe for now and did not appear to bear Thomas any ill will, which fed into his guilt even more so. Sheeva noted that now he was himself he appeared to have the weight of the world on his shoulders. She suspected it was easier to be someone else and hide from his feelings but now it was all stripped away he was laid bare, his identity, his mistakes, his hurt. It was one of the things she loved about him, his willingness to take up a cause and defend those around him. She could not imagine him ever opposing the mixing of magical blood and wondered how much she had known him. Last night she had given into her emotions but the mornings slate sky with its biting cold brought clarity with it. They had escaped but only just, Eli was still out there and the resistance were still being hunted.

Some had left, happy they had survived but unwilling to risk their families again. Thomas did not attempt to stop them, instead he embraced them each in turn, thanking them for their help. Sheeva observed from the corner of the room. How had she not seen it? He moved the same, held himself the same and his eyes... those eyes had convinced her to join the resistance. Seeing them every day had helped somehow, like she had a part of her Thomas. Little did she know she'd never lost him, she'd been fooled just like the rest. Sheeva knew he was powerful but keeping his illusion for so many years took tremendous power.

'What now?' Violet asked, when the last few had left the safe house. She edged into the room, looking excited at the prospect of finally being allowed to use her magic. She and her twin sister Daisy, had been told in no uncertain terms to 'stay put' but Violet was a little too head-strong and her parents knew better than to hope she would be silent for long.

'Now we find Eli before he finds us. We need to regroup, the time for hiding has passed. Those who remain must be willing to stand with us, to come out of the shadows,' Thomas looked around the room, a disgruntled vampire, a stubborn nymph and a portly middle aged couple. It did not bode well that these were the ones most willing to fight.

'Will there be fighting?' Violet wondered curiously, turning her wand around on her hand absent-mindedly. Her mother leant over and snatched the wand away, just as sparks sprung from them knocking a book from the shelf on the far side of the room.

'She takes after her mother,' Thomas grinned, observing his peeved niece. Martha looked outraged for a second before laughing knowingly. 'Not yet. We need someone who will blend in, find those in hiding and send those that would fight. If they have lost faith in our cause so be it, we will leave them be,' Thomas answered.

'I'll go,' Gabby volunteered, 'I can travel during the nights and rest through the day, that way I'll avoid Eli and his goons.' Thomas nodded in agreement. He was pleased she would be leaving, Gabby became agitated when stuck in one place for long. It was best for all of them if she moved on, she could be more help on the road.

'Very well. I'll give you a list of their last known locations in the morning.'

'No. I leave tonight. There is no time to waste,' Gabby said pacing the floor, a predatory look in her eyes which implied she needed to feed. Thomas pulled a rolled parchment from the top drawer of the desk, after whispering a spell, it glowed and letters appeared upon the page before changing to indefinable scrawls and scribblings.

'Only you will be able to read the names and addresses on this list. It has been spelled to you only; a necessary precaution.'

Gabby unravelled it and nodded, 'I will send as many as I can as quickly as I can. When the last have been sent I will return.' She stooped to pick up her bag and without even a goodbye was gone.

'What about the rest of us?' Sheeva asked, 'are we to twiddle our thumbs, shouldn't we send more to recruit?'

'We do not want to attract unwanted attention. Better to move a little slower and be successful then move swiftly and fail,' Thomas concluded. Sheeva could not help but see the logic in his reasoning but she bristled nonetheless. He sounded so much like the Thomas she had known as the resistance leader, it only reminded her of his deceit.

'We must train those who arrive and we need our best warriors for that.' Thomas turned to John and Martha, who looked surprised that he was looking at them.

'Surely the resistance is not so badly off brother, that you'd have us old fuddy-duddy's in charge of defence. I have been without my magic for sixteen years, I am old and slow and as for John, well. He spends half his life napping,' Martha stood hands on hips as though scolding her younger brother, as she had many times before.

'She's not wrong Thomas,' John agreed sleepily. Thomas moved swiftly, a hex exploded from his finger-tips, aimed at Violet. The teenager's face turned ashen as she opened her mouth to scream. Before the sound left her lungs. Martha leapt in front of her, wand drawn she repelled the hex easily. John now wide awake instinctively returned fire, hitting Thomas square in the chest.

'HAVE YOU LOST YOUR RUDDY MIND?' Martha screamed stalking towards her crumpled brother. He was doubled over, a smirk dancing across his lips. Sheeva grinned but quickly hid her smile. Violet looked outraged and excited all at once. Martha just looked outright murderous, she still had her wand trained on her brother.

'I told you. You and your husband *are* the best. Nearly all those who fought alongside you at the council chambers say they owe their lives to you,' Thomas stood, wincing in pain. John shot an apologetic look. 'Magic is part of you, it comes effortlessly. I always thought you were gifted when you were younger but now you're a wonder to behold.'

'Okay. We'll train them. I'll start with those here already and our children,' Martha's eyes met a defiant Violet's. Daisy looked as though she might faint and started fanning herself. Martha shoed her children and husband from the room, Daisy protesting all the way, arguing that she would simply stay out of the way if it came to it.

'Night Uncle Thomas,' Violet darted back and squeezed her uncle, clearly happy to be useful and allowed to use her magic. Thomas froze. He had forgotten for a second that he was an uncle. It had been so long since he had seen his sister. The last time he had seen Martha, she'd just had Zachary. His eyes filled as he thought of his other niece, the one who had lost her father and whose mother was barely alive. He could not help but wonder, if he would ever embrace her again. Would he have the chance to tell her who he really was? And if he did, would she ever forgive him for his lies?

Daisy gave a watery, nervous smile before following

her mother. John motioned to Violet, who skipped back out of the room, leaving Sheeva and Thomas alone again.

Sheeva shifted uncomfortably, being in close proximity was upsetting her plans to keep focused and stay mad at him. No matter how angry she was, it didn't change the fact that she loved him still. Thomas poured another drink for himself.

'What about me?' Sheeva asked, finally breaking the tension.

'We have an equally important task. It will be most dangerous and may not even yield the results I hope but we must try.' His voice was steady and serious and took on the authoritative tone that always instilled confidence in Sheeva.

'Which task?' She asked pacing, unable to look him in his eyes.

'Lithiana is hiding something, we know this now. The intelligence from Fern tells us that much. The answers are within the Village Hall archives, I know it. We cannot afford to sit and bide our time, we must find out about the magic within the bracelet she was so keen to find. I also had hoped that if there were a way to bring them home from that place, we might find answers there also.'

'We cannot simply march on the elves, Lithiana would have the council down on us in a matter of minutes. My cover is blown. Eli knows I am resistance,' Sheeva looked confused.

'My magic will extend to you. I can keep your identity hidden as well as my own.'

'I'm sure they would be wary of strangers after your rescue, we would be found out as soon as we arrived,' Sheeva argued.

'I realise that, I thought we'd adopt familiar personas.' He clicked his fingers and Sheeva gasped as Thomas transformed into Jay. In the mirror, hung atop the fireplace, Sheeva found herself looking into her own, now unfamiliar eyes.

'Okay Jay will be accepted but who am I exactly?' She stroked her long, magenta, spiraled locks.

'You my dear, are Fern's sister Tilda. She left the village years ago but visits on birthdays. So she is not unfamiliar. I will send word to Fern and tell her to expect us imminently.' Thomas whispered and threw a sprinkle of dust into the hearth which sparked and then faded. 'I told her we would be there before morning,' He strode across the room and opened the door. Thomas hesitated at the door sensing Sheeva's trepidation. For the longest time he just stood there waiting, Sheeva stood taking in his latest guise. It really was very clever, if she didn't know better she would swear it was Jay.

'How did I not see it?' She finally said as she made to follow him, her eyes finally meeting his. They were his own for a second before Thomas changed them to Jay's large blue eyes. 'I feel like such a fool,' she said quietly, before sweeping from the room. Thomas lingered for a moment. He knew she must hate him and he couldn't blame her. Being so close to her and being unable to hold her was torture. He sighed and followed Sheeva outside into the dark night.

Chapter 19

Biding Time

It seemed like days since he had heard Helena or anyone else. For a dark moment Jay wished something as wicked and evil as her had swooped down and wiped Helena from existence. He shook the thought from his head, he needed to keep hopeful and embrace his love of Regina if he was to survive this.

The magic he had managed to perform was more powerful than his but still he could not seem to break through the walls. He wondered if somehow he was borrowing some of this new-found power from Regina.

The door to his cell suddenly flung open and Helena sashayed in. This place agreed with her it seemed. Jay looked down at his hands covered in dust and dirt. His injuries had healed quickly, Helena had seen to that but Jay knew she had kept him alive for a purpose and it wasn't out of the kindness of her heart.

'Good. You haven't died, you're no good to me dead elf,' She licked her blood red lips. Jay pushed his back further to the wall, all too aware that he was weak and that he was in the presence of one of the most powerful vampires in history. Part of him felt like rushing for the door and trying his luck. No. He had to be smart. He would hide his powers and bide his time. He needed to give himself and Regina time.

'Why exactly do you need me?' He asked, getting shakily to his feet.

'It speaks! I had thought you'd been struck dumb,' she teased. 'I don't need you, just your blood. Don't worry, I won't kill you … yet.' Delicious smugness flashed across her face.

'You might as well tell me why? It's not like I have anyone to tell besides I'm bored,' Jay declared in his best whiny teen voice.

'What? You think I'm that naïve? You want me to spill my monstrous scheme, like some corny super-villain in a cheap film,' she snorted in disgust, but her eyes glinted. Jay smirked, he had her. She was nothing if not vain.

'Worth a try,' he sighed, his shoulders slumped in defeat. She shook her head as she pulled the door closed behind her. She lingered for a second, hovering indecisively.

'I will tell you this though. You will help me get my family back and when we are together again, those who stand against us …' She trailed off, a hint of sick glee in her voice, as if she couldn't wait to do unspeakable things.

The door slammed and Jay moved from the wall he had been 'leaning' onto. He had used his time wisely. Growing in strength both physically and magically. Much as he wanted to be free of Helena, if her plan was to reunite her family, he had to stop her and when Regina found him, he'd be ready to fight.

Some things had begun to fall into place or at least Jay had begun to figure them out the best he could. He assumed that the man he heard outside his cell, was Helena's husband; if she was getting her family back that would make sense. He knew the tales of her daughter, it had been the stuff of nightmares when he was a young boy; he wondered how much of it was true. He wished for the millionth time that Regina was here with him. He'd spent most of his captivity kicking himself for not telling her how much she meant to him. He knew she liked him but it never seemed the right time to confess his feelings. He was beginning to realise that there would never be a good time, he closed his eyes and prayed; something he never did. It was a human thing to do and his father had never been religious but right now Jay would take any help he could get from anyone.

'Bring her safely to me,' he whispered into the nothingness.

Chapter 20

Double the Trouble

Gabby had been travelling for two nights now and every resistance member she located had been very resistant indeed. She found it ironic at first but now it was irritating. If even *she* was willing to put her neck on the line, what was wrong with the rest of them?

The next name on the list was Jerome and Phyllis Huddleworth. Before Gabby could knock on the pretty red door, decorated with painted flowers, it was yanked open and she was pulled into an embrace.

'Thomas has sent you,' the hugger stated. Gabby pulled herself free, she didn't do hugs. Such an unnecessary human … thing. She shuddered a little. Contact with others, made her uncomfortable especially when it was attached to emotions, urgh!

'He has … and you are?' Gabby asked, taking in two frail and wizened figures. The woman was barely 5 feet tall and hunch-backed. Her hair fell into her face like greying cobwebs. Next to her, a man not much taller with scarcely a hair to his name. Perched on the end of his nose, a pair of glasses so thick that looking through them left Gabby feeling cross-eyed.

'OH HOW RUDE OF US, I'M JEROME AND THIS IS MY SISTER PHYLLIS,' the old man shouted, a high pitch squeal followed. Phyllis rolled her eyes before shuffling over and turning a switch on her brother's hearing aid.

'Better?' She asked.

He nodded, 'Much,' he smiled. Gabby didn't know

what to say, was she supposed to recruit these relics? She pulled her list out and double checked the names and address.

'You are the Huddleworths?' She tried to disguise her disappointment, she was unsuccessful. This was the first home she had been welcomed into and it was by a couple of geriatrics, who looked as though a gust of wind could carry them away. 'Thomas is looking for those still faithful to the cause to return. We have a safe house, you would be more than welcome to join.' She half-hoped they'd complain about their aching joints and turn her down but to her utter amazement, Phyllis clapped her hands and nodded enthusiastically. 'If you wish to go, simply drop this powder. It will take you there,' Gabby said handing the bottle to Jerome.

'Shall we get ready then sister?' Jerome said happily before clicking his fingers and transforming into a tall handsome, young man. Gabby guessed he was thirty something. Gone were the thick lenses and his shiny dome was now covered in thick blonde hair. Gabby gasped in astonishment. She knew there were changelings out there, but they were very rare and most were less than talented. Thomas was very rare and powerful among them and so it was a shock to Gabby. 'That feels so good,' Jerome stretched languidly. His sister grinned mischievously before clicking her fingers and transforming into a thirty something, stunning woman. Her hair was the same shade as her brother, as were her dancing green eyes. She laughed and twirled.

'Thank goodness,' Gabby declared, 'I'm so glad that the first people I send back to Thomas won't be decrepit old biddies.' The siblings, twins she presumed, gave her a hard look. 'What?' Gabby said innocently.

'I can see why Thomas sent you, such ... diplomacy,' Jerome drawled, an icy tone in his voice. Gabby growled an animalistic sound that would send chills through anyone.

'Now, now Jerome. Let's not be catty,' Phyllis chided. 'Tell us of the fight, how does it go?' Phyllis asked turning her attention back to Gabby, who was placated for the moment and had ceased growling.

'Not well,' she answered honestly, 'we are few now. Many are scared to stand. After what happened in Venice and with Regina gone, many lost hope. Some believed that Eli would have to bow to our demands with the hybrid on our side, now she is gone we have nothing. If we do not increase our numbers we won't stand a chance when the council finds us, which could be anytime now,' Gabby covered her mouth looking shocked at what had poured from her mouth.

'Truth spell,' Phyllis said looking sheepish but not sorry in the slightest. Gabby had the feeling these siblings were going to be a handful. However their powers would come in handy, she couldn't deny that.

'It sounds like our new vampire friend could use our assistance sister,' Jerome said excitedly. Gabby shook her head in protest. 'It's settled then. We'll come along with you. I'm sure we can persuade some of those cowards.'

'That's very kind of you but Thomas entrusted this task to me alone. I'm sure he would prefer you get to the safe-house. Perhaps you could help with training?' Gabby suggested.

Phyllis wrinkled her nose at the notion, 'we're changelings what we do can't be taught it's genetic. We will be of no use. No, we'll accompany you.' Gabby started to protest but stopped, she could use the help. After all, witches and wizards were wary of vampires at the best of times. Maybe she would be better received with a magical entourage.

'If you're coming, you have five minutes to grab whatever you need. We have another three houses to try before sun-up,' Gabby snapped, grabbing the spelled list back from Phyllis, who had plucked it from her hand. 'I'm the only one able to read this list, so keep up or get left behind,' she called and burst out into the chilled night. Phyllis and Jerome rushed to catch up, jabbering to one another as they went.

The safe house was at odds with itself. For half of the day, some of the older, injured resistance members taught the younger members, including John and Martha's children all about how to use magic; when not to use magic and which enemies to steer clear of altogether. Daisy, her older brothers Zachary and Francis and her little brother William, relished the chance to use their magic in a fun way and hearing old stories of magical foes. Violet rolled her eyes and counted down the minutes till the afternoon, when she had the chance to learn how to fight and defend herself using magic.

Training started at 12:30 pm sharp and John and Martha ran a tight ship. Trainees paired up whilst Martha observed their fighting stances and gave them advice on the best way to defend. John circled giving them offensive techniques, teaching them how to look for weaknesses in their enemy. They made an indomitable team and as the days passed, most of the older members joined the training too.

Violet was in her element, spinning and attacking with such ferocity that her parents could not help but be impressed and petrified all at the same time. They were certainly glad that she would not be as defenceless as her sister in a fight, but the thought that they were training their children to fight for their lives was never far from their minds.

The days dragged by, everyday Martha was sure that this would be the day they heard from Sheeva or Thomas. She threw herself into teaching, surprising herself by how good she was at it and how much she loved it. Mostly she just wanted to keep busy, she'd lost Regina and now she was afraid she would lose her younger brother all over again.

As twilight hit the surrounding hills and the class had been dismissed, Martha sat on the old bench beneath the tree, watching as the greying clouds chased each other across the sky. She looked at the descending darkness, wondering if Regina was safe and hoping with all her heart, she would find her way home.

D M Singh

Chapter 21

Jay

Sleeping was the only escape from his stifling prison and so Jay slept, fitfully, but still he slept.

In his dream he saw a castle, grand and immense. Surrounded by demons and monsters. A moment later he was inside the castle, face-to-face with Regina. She grinned as he approached, a shy but exuberant smile that could not help but give him hope. She tucked her hair behind her ear and looked up at him through her lashes as he neared her.

'I can't believe it worked,' she breathed, as he stopped just short of invading her personal space. He kicked himself again, even in his dreams he was wussing out.

'What worked?' He asked as she closed the space between them. Her eyes were her own, he was glad to see, no monsters in control of his Regina.

'I brought you here. I'm in trouble. I know I'm here to rescue you but I think this time I'm the one who needs saving,' her eyes pleaded with him as she moved in and threw her arms around him. 'I thought I'd never see you again,' she whispered.

'This feels so real,' he murmured into her hair. Regina pulled away and looked him in the eye.

'That's because it is,' she told him, 'you have to come find me, if you don't … I don't know what might happen,' she shook as she spoke, Jay pulled her back into his arms. He had never seen her so broken before. If this was real, if she was somehow communicating with him, he had to find a way to help her.

'I'm staying with someone called Alexander. He's

159

helping me as much as possible but I need you.' The urgency in her voice pulled at him. She needed him, how he longed for her to say those words to him.

'I can't hold the connection much longer, the spell, it's too strong,' she pulled away and began to fade, he reached out but she was gone.

Jay awoke with a jolt. Cold sweat trickling down his forehead as he took deep breaths, trying to figure out what had just happened.

After pacing for hours, thinking about what he knew and what he had just seen, Jay took a deep breath. He had to get out. He had harnessed as much magic as he could from Regina. He just hoped it was enough to get him out.

'Figyelji,' he whispered, a powerful spell to hear enemies. Nothing. He steeled himself and hoped that his spell had worked. If not, who knew what Helena would do to him? He was stronger than he had ever been but Helena was ancient, only Regina's strength could compete with her.

'Robbanas,' he cried, louder this time and closed his eyes; silently pleading. The door exploded, dust rising into the air, covering everything. Jay coughed and rubbed his eyes before running out to freedom. To Regina.

Chapter 22

Hall of Records

They flew under cover of darkness. The Branches rustled as they passed by gentle leaves that brushed against their skin. The edge of the elven village shimmered into view as they passed through the protective barrier. Sheeva and Thomas passed through easily. Much to Sheeva's relief, Thomas' magic remained intact.

They landed near Fern's dwelling and kept to the shadows, though their disguises were without reproach they could not afford to be reckless. The frayed rope bridge, which led to Fern's door, creaked and complained as they hurried across. Her dwelling, like many of the others, was placed there through a combination of magic and elf ingenuity, and was so high in the trees anyone below would struggle to see it.

Sheeva knocked on the heavy door, eyes darting towards the shadows with every sound. Fern opened the door, looking confused for a second, then hurried them in.

'For a moment I thought it really was him,' Fern said sadly, closing the door firmly behind them. Sheeva added some protection charms after Fern had locked it. Thomas smiled kindly.

Sheeva and he had spoken on the way to the elf village about keeping Fern in the dark about Jay. Sheeva insisted Fern needed to know, if they needed her help, she had to know what was at stake. Besides, she would be more likely to help if she knew it could help save her son. Thomas said little about it but agreed in the end. There had been enough deception already.

'Fern we have to talk about Jay,' Thomas said gently, shedding his illusion as he spoke. Fern started at the sight of this 'stranger', seeing Thomas for the first time as himself. She nodded, suddenly understanding that Thomas had let his guard down, she would be free to see into his mind. She would finally know the truth.

'He's dead, isn't he?' Fern's lip trembled, meeting Thomas' eyes.

'No, not dead, but he is in grave danger.' Sheeva wondered if it would be easier to hear that he was dead. For all they knew he was or would be very soon.

'Then he is lost,' Fern cried, sobs rattling in her chest as she spoke.

'Regina went after him,' Thomas said quickly, 'as did Poppy and Imogen. She believed she could bring him back.'

'Oh poor foolish girl. There's no way back, everyone knows that.'

'There may be a way back,' Sheeva interrupted Fern's despair, 'we have reason to believe that Helena means to return and if she does, that means …'

'There is a way back through,' Fern finished for her, brightening at the thought.

'There has to be a reason she took Jay. We think she did so to lure Regina into The Darkness. Sadly our knowledge about The Darkness only extends to the old myths. However …' Thomas trailed off.

'The archives may have the information we seek,' Fern finished again. 'Well? What are we waiting for?' Fern jumped up heading for the door.

'We have to be clever about this, by now Eli will have informed the elf elders about the resistance attack. We can't do anything to raise their suspicions. We might only get one chance to find what we need,' Thomas said, apology in his voice.

'Which means, no midnight break-ins,' Sheeva added. Fern opened her mouth to object but quickly changed her mind. They were right, if they failed she might never see Jay again.

'So what's the plan?' She asked, slipping into her habit of whipping up some tea and biscuits to occupy herself in the corner of the room which served as a kitchen.

'Elves can ask to access their family records on the archives, so I was thinking it was time your sister ...' Thomas nodded towards Sheeva, 'became curious about her family tree.'

'Once we're in, we'll grab anything we can on The Darkness. We need to be in and out as soon as possible.' Sheeva regarded Fern. She hoped the elf would be able to hold her own if it came to a fight and wondered if she understood what helping them would mean for her.

'Don't you worry about me dear,' Fern said reading Sheeva's thoughts. Sheeva cursed herself, she had been away from them so long she had forgotten to guard her thoughts. 'I know how to take care of myself and I realise I won't be able to return.' She looked around her cosy home with sadness. 'It's hard to believe that so many people have lost their lives and loved ones just because they're frightened of someone a little different. You would think that we magical beings would be more accepting.'

'Pack what you need. We won't be returning,' Thomas said simply, his eyes watching the dying embers of the fire. He would not sleep tonight, none of them would. Fern pottered as if bidding her home goodbye, piece by piece. Sheeva sat in silence, her arm resting on Thomas' and watching the fire. She just prayed it would be worth the risk.

The village hall was deceptively large, a spell long since cast, hid the maze of tunnels and numerous rooms filled with all manner of files, books and magical artefacts. Of all of the magical creatures in existence, elves were the most meticulous record keepers. They had the longest life span, bar the vampires, but given their penchant for stirring trouble with one another and a tendency to get themselves killed, it had been decided centuries ago that the most important records would be kept here.

Thomas had always been curious to see this place. Before the resistance he had been a teacher and the educator in him loved the idea of all this history under one roof. As they approached the small plain door it opened to reveal a cavernous room. An echo carried through the air like an alarm as they closed the door but no-one appeared to notice. Elves hurried back and forth on their way to their offices, or else joining the extremely long queue to apply for access to the records.

At the front of the queue, a vampire was arguing loudly about his need to trace his blood line, to find his creator but the smug looking Elf at the front was immovable and eventually called for security to have him escorted to the village boundaries.

'Can you believe the nerve of some people?' The elf in front of them sniffed. Fern just nodded in agreement. The elves were serious about keeping their records safe, even from others in the magical community. The only ones allowed access were those with permission from the Council of Elders or elves. Elves were trusted mostly due to their reputation for honesty, plus security elves could easily spot those lying; just one look in their eyes and you were done. Thomas took a deep breath and pushed the illusion further. Sheeva felt her eyes burn for a second but didn't say a word. He'd warned her earlier that he needed to protect them both from detection and that this magic came with painful side-effects.

Two hours later, they finally reached the front of the

line. Fern marched straight up to the desk, tapping her fingers as she waited for the elf in charge to help her.

'Can I help you?' She snapped looking harassed and impatient.

'I need to access my family history files,' Fern said quickly. Thomas stepped forwards, pushing the illusion with him as he did. He had never attempted this kind of magic before and he hoped it held long enough to get them in. The elf regarded Fern intently, her eyes searching for deception. She looked confused for a second before nodding and handing her a form.

'Who are they?' She motioned to Thomas and Sheeva.

'This is my son and my sister. My sister no longer lives in the village, so she wanted to do some research whilst here,' Fern said brightly, a smile plastered nervously on her face.

'Come forward,' she barked. She arose from her chair and tottered around the desk to inspect them. She was a tiny elf and had to crane her neck to observe the two elves before her. Her eyes widened, then narrowed looking for deceit. Pleased she saw none, she nodded and returned to her perch. 'Write your names at the top of the form and hand it to the guard in the lift at the end of corridor H. The guard will take you to your record room. You have two hours to complete your research. You may make notes but you are prohibited from making replicas or removing any documents from the archives. Do you understand?' She arched a brow as she looked up from her desk. All three nodded. 'Good, sign at the bottom of the form. This is a contract to say you understand the instructions given, if you break any of the guidelines set forth, you will be liable for damages and detained for prosecution by the Council of Elders.'

'We understand,' Thomas answered in Jay's voice.

'Good... NEXT,' she yelled, indicating they should

move on. Sheeva smiled at Thomas, who gave her a lopsided grin.

The guard was an ancient looking elf who croaked out directions to their record room. They were to find their records on floor 456, room 23F. Thomas and the others followed the directions and entered the correct room, mostly because there were security orbs floating above making sure they did. Once the door was closed Fern pressed her ear to the door listening intently for the telling whooshing noise, which indicted the orbs had been deployed elsewhere.

'Clear,' she whispered.

'What now?' Sheeva asked, anxious to find what they needed and return to the safe house.

'Now we head deeper in,' Thomas answered, 'the oldest scrolls and books are kept on the lower levels.'

'That's right, my neighbour Heather works restoring and preserving them. She let slip once there is a level -1, that's where it would be, I'd bet my best teapot on it,' Fern said, as though using her teapot as collateral made it fact.

'Level -1 it is,' Thomas said, 'Sheeva, would you do the honours?' Sheeva pulled a pouch of red dust from her pocket and blew it across her palm. It circled Thomas, Fern and Sheeva and hung there for a moment.

'Ceil,' she whispered. The dust rose to the ceiling before cascading back down on them all, Fern sneezed in response. A second later they were gone, hidden from view.

'You'll need to shield our thoughts Thomas,' Sheeva said to the nothingness.

'Of course,' he agreed.

Level -1 was very different from level 456. The higher levels consisted of walls made of windows, now and again a record room with solid walls and a door blocked the light. Down here it seemed as though light very rarely made an appearance. The walls looked damp and the corners were so dark Fern worried about what may be lurking round them. They had less than an hour and a half left before they had to be back in the record room, or they would be discovered.

There was an abundance of security orbs on this level. They were obviously in the right place. Doors donning heavy wooden bars lined both sides of the corridor. Thomas shook his head, where to begin?

'There,' Sheeva whispered. Unable to see where she was pointing, Thomas followed the sound of her footsteps. As he neared the end of the corridor, he spotted the door she had in mind. It was the only one which glowed, a sign of extra protection charm and spells.

'I'll take care of it,' Fern said from behind them. Before either could object, they heard a sweet humming. The aura around the door flashed green and then disappeared. 'Nothing to it,' she said quietly. The door swung open and they hurried in. Inside Thomas dropped the illusion and all three popped back into view.

'When we get to the safe house, you have to show me how you did that,' Sheeva said in awe of Fern's skills. Fern simply laughed and started sifting through a filing cabinet labelled dark magical artefacts.

'Got something!' Sheeva exclaimed half an hour later. Thomas dropped the lid of the box he was rummaging through and rushed over.

'What is it?'

'I'm not exactly sure,' Sheeva bit her lip, leafing through a pile of parchments. 'I saw something here,' she tapped the parchment on the table, 'it mentioned a rare magic that was traditionally woven into the very elements of metal. Here it is.' She squinted at the faded calligraphy, it was in Elnian. An ancient language, which was spoken by only a few elves and nymphs. Luckily for them Sheeva was one of them. 'It says … these rare items were usually disguised as jewellery, marked with two distinct symbols, a moon and a sun.'

'Regina was wearing a bracelet like that the last time I saw her. Poppy gave it to her,' Fern piped up, having surfaced from the sea of paperwork she was drowning in. Sheeva nodded and continued reading.

'The potent magic within these charms magnifies the wearer's power. The sun and moon were chosen to represent dark and light magic. When both are balanced, it's a powerful protective charm.'

'Well that doesn't sound like a bad thing perhaps it will enable Regina to find her way out of the darkness,' Thomas said hopefully.

'Wait there's more. If the wearer's magical inclinations are dominated by the dark, the bracelet will fight all traces of light magic within the wearer until it is completely eradicated.' Sheeva's eyes met Thomas' and widened, 'Regina was exposed to dark magic when Aurora attacked the resistance headquarters, if she's wearing that bracelet now and the darkness grows in her ...' She trailed off, taking a deep breath.

'We can't do anything about that, not now at least. We just have to hope that she doesn't succumb to the darkness,' Thomas said a note of sad resignation in his voice, 'grab it and let's keep looking.'

'This could be helpful but it's in Elnian,' Fern held up a file containing sheaves of paper.

'That's odd,' Sheeva remarked, turning them in her hands and inspecting them. 'Records this new aren't written in Elnian anymore. Someone really did not want anyone reading these. Let me see.' She bit her lip whilst scouring the page for something. 'Aha, here. The Darkness has been told to children for centuries as a fable. Although The Darkness is real, the magical community have been led to believe that the story of the wizard and the vampire was untrue and over the years parts have been added to make the tale more dramatic. Davina and Alexander were indeed separated by Alexander's bitterness, which prevented anyone from passing from The Darkness to the Other Place.' Sheeva broke off whispering wordlessly as she searched for anything that could help them. 'There's a warning,' she said, her eyes still on the paper, 'be warned any who seek to open the passageway for they will encounter The Lost; those who have been trapped for generations and have lost all hope, even lost themselves. In The Darkness no light may survive and those who fall into despair become soulless. If any make it to the Other Place, they will be consumed with the dark and evil from within.' Sheeva took a deep breath. Her eyes met Fern's, who looked horrified.

Thomas was silent for a moment, then he was on his feet checking his watch, 'grab it all, we have less than five minutes to get back to the record room, or we'll be discovered.'

Sheeva grabbed the papers and parchments and hastily stuffed them into her bag. She felt Thomas' illusion slip over her as they disappeared from view once more and dashed into the corridor. Security orbs bobbed past as they walked quickly but quietly towards the lift. Thomas reached out and pressed the button for the lift. The doors opened and they stepped in swiftly. Just as the doors began to close, four security orbs activated; flashing and flying towards the lift. Thomas jabbed at the button urging it to go. The doors slammed just as the orbs reached it. Fern let out a sigh of relief as the door closed and they began to move. As soon as they reached their floor, they raced down the corridor, slamming the door on room 23F; their hearts racing as they did. Less than a few seconds later, two guards followed by two security orbs burst through the door.

'Is our time up already?' Fern said with

disappointment. Looking up from the birthing records she was pouring over.

'Do you think we could come back again before I leave sister?' Sheeva piped up from a chair in the corner, tapping a quill on her note filled pad. 'I found most of what I needed. However, Cousin Belle still maintains Uncle Clyde was born here but I couldn't find any information on him,' she pouted. The two security guards watched the 'sisters' interacting and seemed to buy their play-acting.

'Hang on where's the boy? There are three names on this record,' the first guard said. He raised his hand and magic flared across the palm of his hand.

'I'm here,' Thomas yelled from a comfy chair near a stack of books. He stretched and yawned. 'What did I miss?' He said sleepily, rubbing his eyes. 'Please tell me you found what you're looking for Aunty Tilda. I don't think I could survive the boredom if we had to come back again,' he rolled his eyes and Fern smirked. For a middle aged wizard Thomas was playing adolescent elf to perfection.

'Don't be so rude young man,' Sheeva said, clipping Jay around the back of the head, a little harder than she needed to and suppressing a smug grin as she did. The guards at the door exchanged a look and shrugged.

'The building is closing, make your way quickly to the exit,' the guard said. Fern looked confused.

'Why are you closing so early? Is something wrong?' Fern asked innocently as they followed the guards down the corridor.

'Nothing for you to worry about, just an internal matter. If you would make your way out of the building,' he motioned towards the lift. The three stepped on and made their way up and out of the building, none of them dared speak, their hearts in their throats as they quickly exited and crossed the village square.

At the edge of the village, a golden shimmer washed over them as they took to the sky, just as the alarms began to sound.

D M Singh

Chapter 23

Helena

'You have done well,' Helena purred, as she looked out on row upon row of demons, dragons and all manner of nightmarish creatures.

'Thank you mother,' Sophia grinned, looking suitably proud of her own cleverness. 'It all went smoothly, as you said it would.'

'It won't be long now, once we have the girl, we will be a family once more. Nothing will keep us apart again.' Helena pressed her lips to Sophia's cool forehead.

'What of father?' Sophia wondered.

'He will join us as soon as soon as he is able.' Helena saw the disappointment in her daughter's face, 'things must be done properly if we are to succeed,' she explained. Sophia's eyes flashed black but she nodded.

'How are we to find her?' Sophia asked, as she led her mother away from the main chamber of the large fort they had taken residence in. The growls and snarls of the assembled force faded in their wake. She led her to a small bare, windowless room.

'What a horrid little room,' Helena remarked, 'I really don't know why you like it Sophia dearest.'

'I enjoy the peace,' Sophia shrugged, 'so how do you intend to find the girl?'

'Your father has that in hand. It won't be long now. We must be patient.'

'I have been nothing BUT patient mother, ever since you sent me to this hell,' Sophia seethed, her eyes flashing dangerously again. Helena looked hastily away, guilt stabbing her like a knife.

'You know I had no choice,' Helena whispered as her face paled.

'I am sorry mother,' Sophia soothed, 'I realise that. I just grow weary of this place.' Helena nodded, of course she would be frustrated after all this time. It meant nothing. It didn't mean that she would lose control again. If everything went to plan. She would soon be as powerful as her daughter and able to keep her in check. 'But if father knows where this Regina is, why not allow me to fetch her for you?'

'I need to be strong enough to face her. Her powers rival yours, I can't risk losing you all over again.' Sophia looked mutinous at her mother's assumption that Regina could get the better of her but kept her cool and nodded, her jaw set in annoyance.

'When do we make our move?' Sophia asked, smoothing her hands through her long hair.

'You'll know. Wait for my signal,' Helena said simply, before standing and heading for the door.

'You're leaving?' Her eyes filled as she watched her mother leave. Helena sighed, she wondered if Sophia would ever quite be whole again. One moment a monster, the next, nothing but a scared child in need of her mother's reassurance. Helena paused.

'I must return to the elf. For the plan to work all of the pieces must be in the right place at the right time. Your father and I will do our part. You must be ready to move.' As the door slammed shut behind her mother, Sophia threw herself into the nearest chair, white eyes blazing. In the great hall, the assembled army cowered as her screams of pain and hunger reached them.

Chapter 24

The Gathering

Over the next few days, more and more people arrived at the safe-house, so many that Sheeva had to create more rooms to accommodate.

Gabby had done better than they anticipated, nearly sixty witches, wizards, vampire and elves heeded the call to arms and had moved themselves and their families in.

Thomas spent most of his time poring over the translations which Sheeva had provided. Fern usually hovered above him all the while, her face filled with worry. Sheeva threw herself into training their ever growing numbers. Martha had done an excellent job in such a small amount of time, even Daisy, who was a reluctant fighter, could now hold her own. Sheeva pushed down all the new anxieties over the information they'd uncovered, she hid her fear with every well aimed punch and kick. Her spells fired her frustration out into the world. But at night when only she and Thomas remained awake, she could not escape.

'Does Fern understand what it means?' Sheeva asked one night, as Thomas leant against the fireplace swirling the fiery amber liquid in the glass he was holding. It sparked and faded as he raised it to his lips.

'She understands that even if Regina finds him he may already be lost to The Darkness forever.' Thomas slammed the glass on the side table, 'we have to concentrate on what we can do here. I know it's hard, I want nothing more than to bury my head in these papers and figure out how to find them and bring them back.'

175

Thomas closed his eyes, tugging his hands through his tangle of thick auburn hair. When he finally opened his eyes they were full of such anguish and pain that Sheeva found it hard to look at him and so shifted her eyes to the dying flames.

'Isn't there any way we can help them?' Sheeva asked, knowing the answer already, but refusing to give up. Thomas shook his head. 'We need to do something ... I need to do something. I can't just sit here waiting for Eli to make his move and do nothing but worry about Regina. I NEED to do something,' she said desperately. There was a pleading in her eyes that Thomas recognised; he saw it in the mirror.

'Send word to Gabby. She is to return by tomorrow evening. You're right, we have to make a move.' He crossed the room, stopping when he reached the door, 'I just hope we're ready for this.' He said more to himself than to Sheeva as he left.

Sheeva's note had fluttered its way through the window of a north London café, where Gabby, Phyllis and Jerome sat sipping coffee. Gabby had barely scanned her orders, before it turned into a butterfly and flew back out of the window.

By the time they reached the safe-house, most of the resistance had long-since sent the younger members to bed. Phyllis and Jerome were warmly welcomed by Sheeva but Thomas' welcome was a little frostier. Gabby guessed he had a lot on his mind. Thomas quickly filled the three of them in on their intelligence mission to the elf village. Gabby could see why Thomas was so distracted, there was nothing to be done for Thomas' niece, Poppy, Imogen or Jay. As for their own predicament, without Regina's power behind them, they were outnumbered and outmatched.

They all gathered in the main living room of the house where couches and chairs appeared to accommodate the number of people gathered. Violet snuck back downstairs and now hovered in the archway between the kitchen and the living room. Martha scowled at her but said nothing and so she remained.

After a few minutes of hushed whispers and chattering, Thomas and Sheeva entered the room. Silence fell immediately as they took their place in the centre.

'You all know by now things have not gone as we had hoped,' Thomas stated. There was nodding and murmuring. 'We lost Regina, our proof of the council's error and our chance to remove Eli from power. If we are to remove Eli now, our only course is war.' A few looked shocked at Thomas' bluntness, others looked resigned, as though it was what they were expecting to hear.

'We cannot sit and wait for Eli to find us, we must strike first. Once we have removed Eli, we can show the rest of the world the monster he truly is,' Sheeva declared, 'in Eli's office, there are stacks of execution orders, signed by him. Once we release those to the magical community, no-one will question the resistances' intentions.'

'We cannot just jump into this blindly,' Martha said thoughtfully, looking around the room, 'we are outnumbered, if we are to attack, we have to be smart about it.'

'That is where Phyllis and Jerome come in,' Thomas gestured to the twins. Phyllis inclined her head, Jerome curtsied. 'Their parents never registered their powers when they came of age, so as far as the council and Eli are concerned they don't exist. They're our secret weapon.'

'We'll get close to Eli and look for opportunities, times he's unprotected, parts of his routine we can exploit and feed that back to Thomas,' Phyllis interjected.

'As soon as I get the word, we will move on him. Those

of you here tonight, have stuck by me throughout this and I thank you for your loyalty. However I know this is a lot to ask, many of you may be hurt, some may of you may die. If anyone does not wish to fight, feel free to leave with my gratitude for all you have done so far.' Thomas waited anxiously but no-one moved.

'So we're just supposed to sit here, waiting for Tweedle-dee and Tweedle-dumber to find the perfect moment to attack, we can't wait forever. You said it yourself. We can't just sit around waiting,' Gabby argued.

'Don't you worry about that love,' Jerome winked. Gabby growled in response. 'Me and my sis have a way of getting things done, quickly,' he grinned, an unnerving twinkle in his eye.

'Phyllis and Jerome are responsible for acquiring some of the most …challenging intelligence for the resistance over the years. I have faith that they will find a way in within the week.' Phyllis nodded confidently at this assessment. 'Until then, we divide into four teams. Team one will sleep, team two guard duty, team three combat training and team four will hone their magical skills. Martha and John have your assignments and the teams will switch off every six hours. That's all for now, we'll inform you of developments as they occur,' Sheeva instructed. People began gathering around Martha and John to find what team they were in before splitting and joining their cohorts.

Phyllis and Jerome lingered after John led a team outside to begin combat training and Martha led another to the study to practice defensive spells. The other two remaining teams made their way outside for guard duty or upstairs to get some rest.

'Gabby has secured multiple safe-houses for you near Eli's private residence and the council chambers. All of the safe houses have been cleared of their residents.' Thomas handed Phyllis a manila file, 'this contains details of the residents of each house, use their identities to get close and get us in as soon as possible. Be careful not to expose yourself, if you run into any trouble contact us through the usual channels, then disappear. Gabby will accompany you.' Thomas handed Jerome a wad of cash, 'just in case you need to disappear,' he explained. Jerome pocketed the money seemingly unperturbed by any of the events unfolding. 'Good Luck,' Thomas added. Jerome gave a cheeky wink as Phyllis and he left to find Gabby, chattering all the while about who would get to be the woman when they got to the first safe-house.

'You really think they are our best shot?' Sheeva said skeptically, her eyes still lingering after them. She turned her impossibly dark eyes on Thomas, who shifted uncomfortably. Sheeva thought she saw pain in his eyes but then it was gone so fast she was sure it had never been there. Thomas edged away from Sheeva and she furrowed her brow. She was mad at him not the other way around, she pursed her lips in annoyance.

'They'll get the job done,' he said simply. He turned his back to her and gazed out of the picture window, his eyes watching the twilight slowly become darkness. He heard the door open, then slam shut. The sound echoed through him. He knew he was enraging her more but if she couldn't bring herself to forgive him, he had to keep his distance. Years of being so close to her had taken its toll, he had reconciled himself to it. Being near and unable to kiss her and tell her he loved her was a torture of his own making.

D M Singh

Chapter 25
Free

Jay ran for what seemed like hours. He ran faster and further than he thought he ever could. It appeared whatever power he was drawing from Regina was also strengthening him physically. He had no idea where he was going, or how to get there, but still he ran. Away from Helena, away from her cruelty, her schemes and the prison she had kept him in.

Jay had seen little of The Darkness or the Other Place. He had been too weak to even lift his head and look around. He briefly wondered what Helena had done to him and why it had worn off. He was pretty sure he was in the Other Place. He remembered Helena celebrating the fact they had passed through a seam or something along those lines. The Other Place was not as he had imagined. He always thought it was a place of brightness and happiness. This place reeked of despair and hopelessness.

Slumping against a broken wall by the side of a muddy trail, Jay looked up to the sky wondering if he had made a mistake in running. After all, Helena was looking for Regina, maybe he should have been patient. The sky above reflected his mood, fluctuating between the deepest blue he had ever seen and an inky black. He closed his eyes for just a moment as exhaustion finally claimed him. No sooner had he fallen asleep, then he heard Regina's voice as clearly as if she were whispering in his ear.

'Come find me,' Jay's eyes flew open and he jumped to his feet. He had to find her.

'This way Jay,' a different voice whispered. Not Regina's but somehow very similar. Jay spun around searching for the source.

'Who's there?' He cried, 'show yourself.'

'I wish I could,' the voice answered, 'but sadly that's not exactly possible.'

'What do you mean? Where are you? What are you?'

'We don't have time for this Jay. If we're going to save my daughter, you need to find her and soon,' the voice whispered.

'You're Regina's …'

'Mother, yes. So if you don't mind, I'd like to stop gossiping and save my daughter before it's too late.' Jay opened his mouth but Evelyn shushed him, 'I'll explain on the way but for now you need to follow me.' Jay nodded. Considering everything he'd seen in the short time he had known Regina, he had to admit her mother being some weird invisible tour-guide wasn't even the weirdest thing. He grinned to himself as he imagined Regina rolling her eyes at his observation. An ache gripped his stomach just at the thought of her. He shook the thought and hurried down the path Regina's mother guided him towards.

Along the way Evelyn explained that though Regina's quick thinking had saved her life, her soul had in-fact already crossed over. This meant that she had no physical body in this place and had spent her time learning to communicate. She told him how she had followed Regina through the seam before the others and witnessed the changes coming over her, because of the bracelet. Jay simply nodded, each new detail quickened his pace as his fear for her grew.

'One thing I don't understand Jay,' Evelyn wondered as they continued through a large scorched barley field, 'how did you escape Helena?' Jay explained how he had been weak at first and how once Helena's grip on him lessened, he had been able to draw power from Regina just by thinking of her. He grimaced as he said it aloud, it sounded a little creepy even to him. Admitting to Evelyn that he was in essence day-dreaming of her daughter, he reddened at the thought and heard a wisp of laughter as he did, which only made it worse.

'It seems that Helena was correct about one thing. You and Regina are the ones who can break the curse,' she mused, 'as far as I can tell you're one of the few who seem able to use magic or abilities in this place, other than the original magic one who created the curse. You're deeply connected.' Jay chewed on this new information. He didn't really know what it all meant but he was glad of it, their connection had freed him from Helena's clutches.

'We're here,' Evelyn's voice startled Jay. They had been travelling in companionable silence for the past few miles. 'Beyond this ridge there lies a castle. Regina and the others are there.'

'Wait aren't you coming?' Jay asked.

'I can't, I have more to do,' and with that she was gone. Jay suddenly felt very alone as he approached the imposing drawbridge. Just as he was mulling over how to get in, he heard an inhuman growl behind him. He turned slowly and found himself face-to-face with five red eyed creatures, all foaming at the mouth. Their eyes were fixed on Jay, who raised his hands as if to say he didn't want to fight.

The first one leapt, jaws snapping inches from his face.

'Tan-nar,' he cried. His attacker flew backwards knocking two of the others over. His attacker cried out, writhing in agony as he fought invisible flames which burned him from within. One of the creatures took one look at the other agonised comrade and ran. Another two flanked Jay, their inhuman eyes devoid of reason or mercy. The one to his right attacked first. Jay reacted instinctively, leaping into the air, he spun a perfectly delivered roundhouse kick knocking the first down, just seconds before the next attacked. The beast barrelled into

Jay hitting him square in the stomach making it hard to breathe. He landed flat on his back, biting his tongue as he fell, blood spurted from Jay's mouth. He rolled just as they sprang again. Jay was on his feet in an instant, moving faster than he thought possible. His fists a blur, he dodged teeth and claws, before landing a few blows which had them reeling and looking from one to another as if questioning if it was worth the aggravation.

'Zalca,' he cried to the skies. The purple haze above exploded, Jay leapt out of the way and much to his surprise took off. He was flying, something he had been unable to do here. Climbing higher, he flew over the drawbridge, just as the lightening split the ground next to the creatures, setting one on fire and rendering the other unconscious.

'Hello Jay,' a cheerful voice chirped next to him. Jay's heart thundered in response, as Regina swooped right into his arms.

Chapter 26

The Waiting Game

Eli Masters was terrified, not that he would admit it to another living soul. It had been days since the resistance had liberated Thomas. An hour later and he'd have had the locations of all those traitorous whelps, his elite Death Squad would have already dispatched them. He returned to the council chambers the next day, only to find at least ten of his best men had been killed. Twice as many were injured and unfit for duty. Eli had fortified the chambers and his home, he knew it was only a matter of time before they struck again. What else could they do? Thomas and Sheeva would not simply sit back and wait to be discovered, nor would they run. It had gone too far, for both sides.

The oak floor clicked beneath his feet as he marched into the meeting chambers. He had called all the council members for an emergency meeting. He knew it was too late to deny his part in this but he could use it to his advantage. He pushed open the door, nodding in greeting as he entered; all council members were there bar Sheeva. The chambers remained as they had the day of the attack, despite the advice of his personal assistant. Taking in the looks of horror on the faces of his fellow council members, he knew it was the right choice. Lithiana leant against what had previously been her seat. Not a single piece of furniture remained intact, splintered wood lay strewn across the floor. Lithiana's eyes were fixed to the puddles of blood on the floor and bloody hand prints daubed up the walls. Her face paled as she swallowed hard.

'My fellow council members,' Eli bellowed from the centre of the room, 'as you can see from the state of this room and indeed the rest of the council building, the resistance has become a serious threat.' His voice carried through the room greeted with silence and solemn faces. 'First, they hide this … monster of a girl, who has done god only knows what with Helena. Now they attack our very way of life; hitting us here, the very place we make laws, where we keep our world safe. They are reckless and they must be stopped. How long before they begin attacking innocent people in the streets, or expose us to the humans? We must act now, we cannot allow this to go unanswered. Good men and women lost their lives defending this room, spilling their blood on this very floor. No. This cannot stand.' His voice rang out, several of the council nodded enthusiastically.

'But what can we do that is not already being done Eli?' Lithiana asked.

'First of all we must discredit these traitors, they paint themselves as heroes fighting for justice,' he paused his voice growing quiet, 'I see no evidence of heroes here, I see barbarians. Those who think they can get their way through intimidation and violence. I have released a worldwide broadcast naming the few members we know to be involved and offering a reward for any information which leads to their capture. But I can do little more than this. According to our laws my hands are tied. I have to abide by the laws of our people and the law is clear. I cannot use excessive force against anyone.'

'Surely not!' A werewolf exclaimed looking around for confirmation.

'It is true,' Lithiana stated, 'you have to remember Janus, we have had no wars or opposition for hundreds of years. No-one person has that authority … not unless the council members unanimously vote the chair to have sole authority during these troubled times.' She watched Eli carefully; he avoided her eyes looking shocked at the idea.

'There must be another way?' Eli countered, 'we have always worked this way, to change things now, well... it wouldn't feel right.'

'Desperate times,' Lithiana said simply, 'I propose we disband the council for the foreseeable future, whilst we capture the resistance.' Hands quickly shot in the air in favour. 'It's unanimous,' Lithiana said quietly, a note of sadness in her voice, 'the council is no more.'

'You have my word that I will find every last one of them and bring them to justice and then my friends, we will serve together once more.'

They left quickly, unwilling to linger in a place filled with the smell of death. As the last of the council members left closing the door behind him, Eli smiled.

'Have you seen this?' Martha burst through the door of the study and slammed a scroll on the desk in front of him. Thomas scanned the page, pictures of Sheeva, Martha and John filled the page with the words traitors and murderers, splashed across the top. 'They've twisted everything. There's no mention of Eli capturing and torturing you. They've even accused Regina of murdering Helena.' Martha paced up and down anxiously. 'That's not even the worst of it,' Martha pointed to the bottom corner. A picture of Eli looked up at Thomas. The headline read *Eli Masters named as Grand Counsel.*'

'This complicates things. I'll contact the twins and see if they can push things along. We need to get control of this before they have the whole country hunting us,' Thomas tugged his hands through his hair, a faraway look in his eyes.

'What does this mean for us?' Martha worried aloud, 'Eli with complete power,' she shuddered. 'He murdered our parents without complete control, I can't even imagine what he can get away with now, especially since he has made us public enemy number one.'

'Let's hope we get a chance to show the world, who the real monster is before too many people get hurt,' Thomas sighed. Martha grabbed the scroll and stomped from the room, swearing at Eli under her breath.

It was two days before they received word from Gabby. The message was vague but the instruction was clear. They should be ready to attack the following night. Thomas and Sheeva kept the group divided, deciding that they would be wiser to attack in small teams. The faster they gained control, the quicker this could all be over. They could set the record straight, remove Eli from power, maybe even get the elf's to help them figure out how to rescue Regina, Jay and the others.

Thomas, Sheeva and Gabby would each lead a team. Martha and John would lead the final team, they fought so well together that it seemed prudent to keep them together. Violet and Daisy would remain behind, much to Violet's dismay. Thomas explained to the twins that as the eldest, they would be in command and responsible for the rest of the children. Violet seemed appeased by this and immediately began planning defence strategies and escape routes with her sister. Martha and John's eldest children, who were just as skilled as their parents in combat, were to join their team. There were tearful farewells, back slaps, embraces and kisses as they made to leave.

Once again they left under the cover of darkness. Gabby and the twins were to meet them below the bridge between the council chambers and Eli's residence. As the teams left in swirls of black and purple smoke from the travel potions, Thomas looked back at the place that had begun to feel like home. This was the first place he had been his true self in over sixteen years. He couldn't help but wonder what would become of those who followed him if things went south and he wondered if he would ever make up for his past mistakes. A hand grabbed his, sparks danced from his fingers and up his arm. He turned to see Sheeva, her eyes filled with panic just as he was sure his were but something in her face told him he was not alone and for a second he allowed hope to creep in.

'Come on Thomas, let's go kick Eli's butt,' Sheeva ground out, her eyes now filled with determination.

'You always say the sweetest things,' he teased, before shattering the travel potion on the ground, engulfing them in a cloud of black smoke.

D M Singh

Chapter 27

Declaration

Jay sat in the large library for over an hour listening as Poppy tearfully explained what was happening to Regina. Jay in turn told them all about his growing powers and strength, how Regina came to him in a dream and finally how Evelyn led him to Alexander's castle.

'That makes sense,' Alexander mused, 'if your connection was strong enough to break through the seal, it makes sense that you would remain connected.'

'In my dream Regina seemed to think I could save her. Can I?' Jay looked hopefully from Poppy to Alexander. Poppy bit her lip, avoiding his eyes, Alexander shrugged looking skeptical.

'We have been looking for some way to help her and to stop the barbs spreading. So far I've found very little,' Alexander said.

'I did find one thing this morning,' Poppy pulled a large red book from the table, 'it says… once the light or dark has run its course, the afflicted one may be reached but only after their heart has been filled.' She looked worriedly at Alexander who shook his head.

'So we can help her, it say's…' Jay began.

'It says before we can help her, her heart must be filled. If that darkness fills her heart who knows what she might be capable of? We know Regina would never hurt anyone unless she had to but I don't think she'll be in control if we let it reach her heart,' Poppy argued.

Jay's restlessness got the best of him. The hopelessness palpable; like a living thing. He jumped to his feet and headed for the door.

'Where are you going?' Alexander asked a note of pity in his voice that angered Jay.

'I'm going to talk to Reggie. She seemed to think I could rescue her, maybe she knows something you guys don't.'

'I'm afraid you won't get much out of her. She's pretty far gone,' Poppy said her eyes shining with tears again.

'I have to try,' Jay reasoned, before hastily leaving the room.

The east wing of the castle looked long abandoned. A grand but dust riddled spiral staircase led the way to the tower. Regina spent most of her time there lately as the spell Alexander cast had begun to lose its hold on her. Jay took a deep breath, remembering the promise he'd made himself about telling her how he felt. He still hadn't worked up the nerve, since he'd arrived Regina had spirited herself away here whilst he was promptly removed to be filled in on her 'condition'. The door creaked open, announcing his presence. Regina was leaning out of the far window, her dark hair tangling around her shoulders as the wind blew through the arched window. She turned and as her eyes met his, Jay smiled. The smile that always lifted her out of whatever hole she was in. It stunned her for a second. She'd barely had time to think about Jay since the barbs of darkness had taken hold. Between the spell and her lucid moments, it took every ounce of strength to hold onto herself. Now he stood before her and her heart started to dance.

'I was hoping you'd come find me,' she said softly. Her voice had changed, Jay frowned. She was weakening, he could hear it.

'Well of course I did. You invaded my dreams, I couldn't not come,' he smirked, 'that would just be rude.' His heart warmed as he was rewarded with a weak smile. She rubbed her arms and Jay flinched seeing the barbs he had heard about. Her wrist still red with blood.

'Why aren't you healing?' He stalked across the room and grasped her wrist.

'It bleeds as they spread,' Regina pulled her wrist away, scared by the intensity in his eyes.

'Doesn't blood heal it?'

'I haven't been drinking it,' Regina said quietly, knowing he would not like it. His eyes widened in disbelief. 'Before you start lecturing me like you're my mum, listen to me.' Jay nodded reluctantly. 'I discovered that the more I fed my immortal side the faster the darkness spreads. So I've stopped. That's why I'm up here like Rapunzel the serial killer,' she scoffed. 'I can't trust myself right now. I'm losing myself Jay.' She raised her eyes to his and they were awash with tears. His heart broke for her. This girl he loved, who had lost so much and yet still kept fighting, for her friends, her family, for the right thing. This girl who never thought of herself, who carried the weight of the world on her shoulders and still managed to be the most caring person he had ever met. His heart swelled as he pulled her into his arms, tensing at her breath against his neck.

'I trust you,' he whispered against her hair.

'Well that makes you an idiot,' she spat, extricating herself from his embrace. Her eyes flashed for a second before they returned to her normal deep green ones.

'Go Jay,' she quivered as she spoke, as if every inch of her was fighting her instinct to kill. He moved towards her again, his hand outstretched. 'NO!' She barked, her eyes black again. 'Go before it's too late,' she begged. Jay nodded and left the room, and as he closed the door behind him he heard Regina sobbing as if her heart was breaking.

Sleep did not come quickly that night for Jay. He tossed and turned, with just one thought in his head; he'd let her down. She'd risked her life, her very soul to come find him in this place. Yet he was helpless. How could he rescue her as she had begged him to in his dream? Sure he was stronger now but what did that matter if she was lost. None of it mattered. As the purple hues faded to deep black outside his window his eyes finally closed.

'Jay?' The sun illuminated the room they stood in. Jay spun around. Regina grinned and leapt into his arms.

'How?' He whispered.

'The darkness seems to recede when I sleep. I'm more in control,' she shook her head, as if she didn't quite understand it herself. 'How did you find me?' She wondered aloud.

'Your mother led me here.' He explained how Evelyn had scared him half to death before explaining who she was. Regina's face dropped at the mention of her mother.

'What if I can't save her? I know I have my dad back but I'm still not any closer to knowing what happened to her or how to get her back. Did she say anything that could help?' Hopeful eyes met Jay's but he shook his head slowly.

'Trust you to be thinking of saving someone else when you're clearly the one who needs help,' Jay watched her face carefully, examining every part. Her glittering eyes, her soft skin. His eyes lingered on her lips. 'I need to tell you something,' he choked out, dragging his eyes away from her lips back to her eyes. He opened his mouth to tell her but words escaped him. She was everywhere, her scent, her smile, her eyes...

'That's funny, I have something to tell you,' she breathed, but before she could say another word, his lips crashed onto hers. Regina gasped, returning his kisses desperate to be near him. She broke the kiss abruptly, stopping it as suddenly as it had begun; reigning herself in. Jay looked hurt and confused. It pained her to see it but she could not let her emotions get the better of her. She couldn't risk it.

'What's wrong? I thought...' He floundered, his big eyes so trusting and full of love. She saw it clearly now. He loved her, it really was written all over his face. She just hoped that it wasn't written on hers.

'I can't,' she stated firmly.

'You can't what? It was only a kiss Reggie. I wasn't proposing,' Jay's voice sang with hurt.

'Exactly,' she said in her most Helena-like voice, 'just a kiss, nothing more.' She bit her lip as she turned away. A tear rolled down her face. She had thought for a second she could be normal. That she could have love; she could have him. The moment their lips met, her monster had awoken, she felt it. This darkness inside of her, craved Jay. She had brought him here to tell him how she felt but she couldn't risk his life.

'You don't mean that,' Jay said confidently, 'I'm not stupid Reggie. I know you. You're trying to push me away to protect me. You did it before but I won't let you do it this time. If you want me out of your life, you'll just have to kill me,' he challenged.

'That's exactly my point,' she screamed in frustration, 'you're joking about me killing you but that is a REAL possibility. I'm not the only one who wants you.' She trembled, trying to keep control. She hated feeling so weak. Jay looked confused. Before he had time to wonder for too long he felt her breath against his cheek, he looked around but no one was there.

'What the …?' He wondered whipping around. Regina's face fell.

'WAKE UP JAY!' She screamed.

Jay's eyes flew open, the breath was still on his cheek. Regina or some version of her sat beside him on his bed. Her blank, white soulless eyes watching him, grinning as his eyes met hers. Jay froze, he knew he could be dead in a moment if she wanted it that way. He swallowed hard.

'Why do you love her?' The voice asked. It came from

Regina but it was not her and Jay wondered if it was too late. Had the barbs reached her heart already? He sat up, his eyes never leaving her face.

'I've never met anyone like her,' he said honestly. Saddened that if she decided to kill him, this could be his only chance to confess his love. 'She's strong and funny. She's beautiful but she doesn't really know or care, she laughs at my ridiculous jokes,' his mouth curled into an involuntary smile just at the thought of her. 'She has a huge heart, she's… magnificent.' His eyes met Regina's monster, they stared at him, unblinking. Jay waited to die.

'Then why won't you save her?' The monster wondered.

'That's why I came, she called to me?' Jay looked confused. Why would her inner demon want her cured of this new darkness?

'She grows weak, she needs blood. Yet you sit there and do nothing,' It accused.

'She refuses to drink the blood. She says it makes the darkness swallow her faster,' he reasoned.

'Not the blood from the fountain. Yours.'

'She would never drink from me. She would worry she might kill me,' Jay explained, wondering how any of this was possible. How was this monster talking, reasoning?

'But I would,' it said simply, 'unless you're worried I would kill you,' its voice cooed, making Jay's skin crawl. He considered his options. If he refused she could very well kill him anyway. He nodded slowly. Regina's monster eagerly inched forward and grabbed his arm before sinking its fangs into his wrist. Jay winced in pain but it subsided after a moment or two.

'She needs more,' Regina's monster stated after retracting its fangs, 'but I can't guarantee I will be able to stop.' Jay was even more confused now.

'Why do you want to help her?' He asked. 'I would have thought darkness in her heart was right up your street. No offense.'

'She IS me. If she is destroyed, so am I,' it said simply, before rising from Jay's bed-side and leaving the room. Jay let out the breath he had been holding, he just hoped Regina would forgive him, once she knew what he had done.

D M Singh

Chapter 28

Last Hope

Ebony rippled across the Thames as a sharp biting breeze reminded Thomas that summer was long gone. Sheeva shuddered and unconsciously moved closer towards Thomas. He instinctively put his arm around her and surprisingly she didn't object. They had been waiting for half an hour and some of the resistance were growing restless, eager to be out of the cold and away from the eyes of humans.

'Sorry about the wait loves,' Jerome trilled, appearing suddenly behind them.

'Where's Gabby?' Thomas asked, looking hurriedly around, 'and Phyllis?'

'Gabby and Phyllis are in position at the council chambers. We need as many there as you can spare,' Jerome said, looking at Thomas, who nodded and indicated two of the teams to follow Jerome. 'I'll be back for the rest of you, then we'll head to Eli's residence,' he added, before disappearing once more with half their number in tow. 'Let's get going then,' Jerome said appearing again in his customary pink swirl of travel smoke.

'What's the plan?' Thomas enquired. Sheeva shot him a look which told Thomas that she was uncomfortable at his taking orders from this peculiar pair.

'Two pronged attack. Alpha team will hit the residence and capture Eli. Beta team will infiltrate the council chambers and secure evidence proving Eli's illegal activities.' Jerome was suddenly focused, a soldier, in complete control, much to Sheeva's surprise.

'Why now?' She asked.

'Eli has been very careful since the attack, he has a guard of at least five at all times. Not the usual guards, these are his most devoted and ruthless Death Squad captains. We have intelligence that he has sent three of his guard to the council tonight to retrieve important documents. So…'

'They'll only be two guards with him, the others will be at the council chambers,' Sheeva finished for him. 'Not a bad plan but how do we get near? If he even suspects we're near, he'll high-tail it.'

'That's where Thomas and I come in. Time to put that changeling magic to use Tommy boy,' he grinned. Thomas grimaced, bristling at the name. Jerome took in the height of the powerful changeling wizard and smiled sheepishly. 'At his residence, Eli has two guards masquerading as human security guards. We take them out and take their place.' Sheeva recoiled at the idea of *taking them out*.

'No killing unless it is absolutely necessary,' Thomas hissed at the two teams.

'You are kidding?' Jerome seethed, 'you know what they've done to people like us, all the people he's killed; the blood that's on that man's hands. You saw what he's capable of, you promised…' Jerome trailed off, glaring at Thomas a look of disbelief in his wide blue eyes.

'Now is not the time for that,' Thomas soothed. Sheeva and those around looked confused. 'If we kill, we are no better than him and his Death Squad.' Jerome nodded jerkily, defiance still glinting in his eye.

Eli's building was three storeys high, with his penthouse running the entire length of the top floor. Sheeva and the remainder of the team were to wait a safe distance away until they were signalled. Thomas insisted that if they had not heard from them within ten minutes they were to join the other teams and help retrieve the proof from the council chambers.

The harsh wind had turned to rain, and fog had already begun to roll in from the river. Thomas and Jerome were cloaked from view as they approached the building. The scarlet door creaked open and Thomas held his breath. The cloaking was enough to get them in, but if they were to get close to Eli without spooking him, they had to work fast. The entrance was swathed in thick carpet which hid their approach as they made their way towards the security desk, where a werewolf (by the smell of him) and a vampire sat. The werewolf was big, bigger than Thomas, which was saying something. At six foot five, he was not often overshadowed by anyone. The vampire had his feet on the control panel of the desk and appeared to be checking his phone every couple of seconds. They knew it would not be long before both the guards picked up their scent, the cloaking spell hid their essence a little but not enough. Before Thomas had time to turn to Jerome, he was gone. Thomas spun around to find him approaching the vampire from the left. Great, thought Thomas, that leaves me the big guy.

'Cur isteach,' Thomas whispered and the radio on the reception desk and phials of potions glowed, before exploding. Shards of glass rocketed through the air and crashed to the floor. The werewolf was on his feet; nose in the air searching for a scent.

'Two of them,' the werewolf growled, his heightened senses scouring for more signs of the intruders. Jerome swung for the vampire just as he caught his scent, a guttural, inhuman sound emanated from his chest, sending a shiver through Thomas. He really did hate vampires, so arrogant and full of pride. Jerome's fist connected with the vamp's chin but had little effect. The vampire spun, his fist slamming into Jerome's chest,

Thomas heard a crack which told him Jerome more than likely had a broken rib or two, but he knew he could hold his own. He couldn't afford to become distracted.

The werewolf leapt across the entry way and landed heavily in front of Thomas a wide grin spreading across his face.

'I'm going to enjoy this,' he grunted as he swung at Thomas, who ducked causing the werewolf to stumble. He recovered his footing, his face now a shade of scarlet. Thomas fired a spell at the wolf, it landed squarely on his shoulder and the wolf cried out in pain, staggering back a few steps. Thomas took advantage and fired a barrage of spells at his chest. The floor shook as the giant crumpled to the ground.

'Well that was easier than I thought,' he shrugged.

Jerome was a blur of faces and shapes as he switched guises between each blow dealt. The vampire stumbled back a look of disbelief flitting across his face. Thomas smirked, Jerome and his sister were very talented, even if they did enjoy causing trouble a little too much. Jerome finally came to a stop. Back to his face, his body, his voice once more. The vampire clutched his chest, mouth gaping as Jerome winked.

'Missing something?' He sniggered, holding up the vampire's heart.

'Jerome,' Thomas cautioned, his wand levelled at him. Jerome rolled his eyes.

'Relax Thomas, I'll leave it here for someone to find. He'll be fine,' Jerome drawled placing the shrunken husk on the security desk.

'Eww!' Jerome cried, wiping his gooey hands on the fallen vampire 'gross!' He scowled at the vampire. 'How'd you knock out shaggy dog there?' He nodded to the wolf that was now snoring loudly.

'He was as dumb as he looked. Come on let's get them out of sight.'

They dragged the guards behind the desk and placed the heart in a desk drawer. Before walking into the lift, both men changed into one of the fallen guards.

'Man! he really is dumb looking,' Jerome commented, observing Thomas' new guise as the door closed and the lift began to ping its way upward. Thomas remained silent, he knew it was Jerome's way to mock everything, rather than face the severity of the situation. The lift jerked to a stop and the doors slid open. The two intruders exchanged a look before stepping out, the doors closing behind them.

'That's it,' Jerome whispered, nodding towards a sleek looking modern door. It looked out of place, Thomas figured it was installed for security reasons. 'Every day at this time the guards from downstairs switch with the two in Eli's flat.'

Thomas took a deep breath before rapping his now hairy knuckles on the door. On the other side of the door they could hear the sound of footsteps and the scraping of bolts. The door shimmered turning from sleek metal to an arched dark mahogany door. Protective spells and illusions Thomas guessed. The door opened a crack and a guard peered out into the hall.

'It's the relief team sir,' the guard from the door called. Eli grumbled something unintelligible from another room and another guard emerged from the room containing Eli's grumbles. Both had wands strapped to their thighs as well as a gun, which answered Thomas' question of who they would be facing, wizards.

'We have swept the residence, all clear,' the second guard informed them.

'Good,' Jerome answered in the voice of the obnoxious vampire. His cold, dead eyes boring into the guards.

'The next relief team will be here in eight hours. Their photos are in the packet by the door, if anyone else approaches the door other than us or the next relief team, kill them,' the first guard said coldly. Thomas shifted, uncomfortably disgusted by how a fellow wizard could be so callous and cold. Jerome nodded stiffly. Upon reaching the hallway, Thomas took out his wand and stunned the guards as they turned to leave. Jerome quickly cast a cloaking spell over them.

'You signal the others, I'll make sure Eli stays where he is,' Thomas said, walking round the room, casting containment spells as he went. He pushed open the door to the study to find Eli mulling over some papers on his desk.

'Yes?' He snapped barely looking up from the papers.

'Just checking in Sir,' Thomas responded, 'do you need anything?'

'To be left in peace,' he spat out, finally looking up from his work.

'Of course Sir,' Thomas left the room, to find one team already in the main living area.

'Where's Sheeva's team?' Thomas asked suddenly panicked.

'Relax big guy, Sheeva and the others are taking care of the guards. They're … relocating them as we speak. I think we can handle Eli between us. What's the plan?' Jerome asked. They had been joined by Thomas' team which consisted of Tom the inn-keeper from the resistance headquarters, a vampire and two witches who had been recruited just a few days ago.

'As far as I can tell there is no way out of the room, I didn't detect any spells. If we knock him out before he can disappear, this just might work. You two watch the front door,' Thomas pointed at the two witches, who nodded and left to take their place at the door. 'You two watch the study door, Jerome and I will take care of Eli. If we're not out in five minutes, rendezvous with the others as planned.'

Eli's quill scratched noisily across the paper on his desk

as the two guards entered.

'WHAT NOW?' He shouted impatiently, looking up at them. Thomas noticed that his face was paler and more drawn than usual.

'There's been a message from the council chambers,' Thomas said smoothly, ignoring Eli's deadly glare. 'The resistance mounted an attack. They were unsuccessful of course. The Death Squad have Sheeva and Thomas in custody.'

'I knew that arrogant idiot wouldn't have the sense to run and hide. We'll head for the chambers now.' He stood and turned his back for a second to gather his things, it was all Jerome needed. Eli didn't have time to defend himself from the spell and he fell to the floor with a look of surprise etched on his face.

'Have we heard from the others?' Thomas asked as they headed out and into the lift.

'Sheeva made contact, we have infiltrated the council successfully but the Death Squads have sent for reinforcements. We need to go now before it's too late!' Tom advised.

'Well it's a good job that we're in control of the man who holds all the power, isn't it?' Jerome smiled, before muttering a few words in the unconscious Eli's ear, who promptly opened his blank eyes, before getting to his feet.

'What have you done?' The smaller witch demanded, looking terrified.

'Don't worry,' Jerome said casually slapping Eli's back, 'old Eli is under my control, he will do and say whatever I want him to.'

'And how will we get into the chambers?' She asked, still suspicious.

'We're going to walk right in,' Thomas smiled.

D M Singh

Chapter 29

Loss

Alexander made his way to his bedroom as soon as everyone headed for bed, waking Emile, who was dozing in the chair beside Davina's bed. Emile stretched and headed for his own room, leaving Alexander to his solitude and silence. He popped the buttons of his shirt and slid it off laying it carefully on a chair near the oversized, ornate wardrobe.

Davina slept fitfully in the days since she collapsed and any effort he made to rouse her had proven unsuccessful. Alexander satisfied his need to be near her by pacing beside her bed every evening, after combing through books with Poppy all day. She lay in his four-poster bed, her bright red curls dancing across the black pillows as the wind blew in through the open window. At first Alexander had placed Regina in charge of Davina's well-being, until the spell had run its course. Now Imogen, Emile and Dragmir took turns sitting with her while they worked tirelessly to find something, anything that could help Regina. Though no-one said it, they all knew there was more at stake than one life. If Poppy, Imogen and Jay were to return, they needed Regina. Without her, they were stuck here.

'Alex?' Davina's soft voice reached his ears as a welcome melody. He was at her side in a heart-beat. Her eyes fluttered open, locking on his, 'is it really you?' She breathed.

'Yes my love, it's me,' His eyes devoured her, moving ravenously across her features. 'I have missed you,' he leant in and kissed her gently on the forehead. She stirred beneath him trying to sit. 'Easy my love, you've been asleep for a while. Take your time.' She nodded and gingerly sat up.

'I never thought I'd see you again,' her voice just above a whisper, 'what happened? Where am I?'

'You had a shock. Your new friends brought you here,' he explained. Davina looked thoughtful.

'I think I remember... We were trying to find a boy... an elf and...' her eyes snapped up, meeting his, 'it was you,' she accused suddenly looking sick. 'You did all of this. Dragmir told me and...' She broke off, her face scrunched as she searched her memories. 'She's gone,' Davina jumped from the bed, panic in her eyes.

'Who's gone?' Alexander said full of concern.

'Baby, she was here and then Dragmir told me that is was you that caused all of this.' She turned from him, her breath came in shallow gasps as her eyes filled with tears.

'She's gone,' she cried, as the tears broke loose. 'You trapped me and everyone else in that place, turned this place into some kind of hell and you killed the best part of me.' She fell to her knees, burying her head in her hands as she grieved for her friend. The one who had kept her safe from The Darkness and from herself.

'I don't expect you to forgive me or even understand what I did,' Alexander said above her soft sobbing, 'I was in such as dark place back then. I became so bitter and I guess it spread. I never expected it or planned it, no matter what the legend says. When I realised what was happening I tried to find a way to reverse it but I was too late. It was all I could do to spread whispers amongst the elves who came here and returned as nymphs in the mortal world. The legend was born. My magic was weak at first but I was able to use it to ensure it wouldn't be forever.' Davina raised her head, her eyes met his and something stirred within him. A love that could not die, would not die, refused to die. 'You know me Davina. Better than anyone ever has. I would never have purposely caused so much pain. I grieved for you, for our love … this was the result. I don't know how or why.'

'Is she gone forever?' Davina croaked, her throat raw from crying.

'You say she was the best part of you?' He asked. Davina nodded. 'Then she is still right here.' He knelt beside her and placed a hand over her heart, the other cupped her tear-stained cheeks. Davina placed her hand over his. Her eyes softened sending Alexander's heart rabbiting.

'I have missed you Alex. I have done such things, I thought I had lost myself,' her eyes glistened a mixture of sadness and relief.

'You'll never be lost again my love,' he promised solemnly, 'you're home.' She crawled into his arms and for the first time in over a thousand years, she felt like she was.

D M Singh

Chapter 30

Compliance

Floorboards creaked and groaned outside the door as Sheeva strained to hear what was coming for them down the hallway. Dreading that this time they would not be able to hold them off. The vampire from her team had fallen quickly and though she would be fine once she had fed, it meant they were down to fourteen against the entire might of the council. She closed her eyes and prayed to the ancients that Thomas would be here soon. Of course she wanted him to save them, but mostly she just wanted him here with her. If she was to fall she wished to do so by his side. She knew she'd been stubborn these last few weeks and she kicked herself for letting her temper get the better of her. If she had swallowed her pride, they could have had a small measure of happiness together.

'Hindsight, always there to kick you in the behind,' she muttered under her breath. Phyllis looked at her confused but shrugged turning her attention back to her team, who were discussing the best counter-curses to use against werewolves.

Martha and John held their own well as Sheeva had known they would. She had a feeling there was more to it than just skill, an aura she had never seen before surrounded them both as they dispatched their enemies.

Phyllis was more than handy in a fight, though some of the spells she used felt very close to dark magic.

They'd been barricaded in Eli's office for over ten minutes now and so far they had failed to locate the files. Sheeva glanced at the carriage clock sat on the mantle, five more minutes; that was all they could afford to give Thomas to show. The Death Squad reinforcements would arrive any moment and Sheeva knew they would most likely not survive another attack.

Scuffles and cries from the other side of the door broke through Sheeva's contemplation. Phyllis, Martha and John were swiftly on their feet, their eyes glued to the door. Sheeva swallowed hard, her breath ragged as her heart pumped faster and faster.

'This is it!' Sheeva said forcefully, her eyes dark and determined. Smoke wisped beneath the door and hovered for a moment, changing from green to red. Sheeva's eyes widened. 'Take cover!' She yelled, rolling across the floor before leaping over the leather couch and shielding her head with her hands. For a moment all was silent, then the world shook and a tidal wave of grey dust swept the room. Sheeva clicked her fingers and light danced across her palm. Taking a deep breath she dove from behind her cushioned haven firing light bolts as she did, barely missing the shadowy figures who had entered the room.

'Hold your fire,' a voice came muffled through the rubble and fog. Sheeva cautiously retreated to her hiding place. 'Sheeva?' The voice was clearer now and familiar and the sound of it brought tears to her eyes. She threw herself into Thomas' arms raising her eyes searching for his sure and steady ones in the chaos.

'Now, now,' Jerome wagged his finger, as he swept past, 'they'll be time for canoodling later but for now let's get what we came for and leave. Shall we?' Sheeva knew Jerome was kidding as usual but still she pushed herself away, embarrassed she had forgotten herself for a moment. She was responsible for getting her team out safe. *'Focus now, Thomas later,'* she reprimanded herself silently.

'They're not where I expected,' Sheeva said as she strode across the room and pulled out the hollowed book where Eli had always kept his most secret documents. She opened it and shook it pointedly. 'We tried a locator spell but it was blocked. I think Eli performed a blood bind, so without him...' Sheeva stopped mid-sentence as Eli Masters strolled into the room, looking a little dazed. Martha was on him in an instant, John at her side.

'Calm yourself,' Thomas soothed his enraged sister, 'he's quite docile at the moment, in fact he'll be more than happy to help us, isn't that right Eli?' Eli nodded dumbly, a glazed look in his eyes.

'Eli?' Sheeva asked cautiously. 'Where are the death squad records pertaining to the ordered torture and execution of Regina's grandparents?' Eli snapped his head up and marched toward the book Sheeva had declared empty. He grasped a letter-opener briefly before slashing his palm.

'*Deschis pentru mine,*' he murmured, over and over. Acrid smoke rose from the spine and a compartment popped open. Eli reached in pulling several scrolls and a manila file out, before turning mechanically and handing them to a shocked Sheeva.

'How long will the spell last,' Sheeva asked.

'He's tied to my will, so let's see, until he stops being an evil psycho,' Jerome said proudly. Sheeva's eyes met Thomas' for a second, he frowned as if he knew what she was thinking.

'What now?' Sheeva asked, a little shocked they had actually prevailed.

'Now, Eli will be releasing a world-wide statement confessing to his misdeeds, he will formally admit that Regina is not to be feared, he will call off the hunt for her and present the proof of his involvement in the deaths of countless resistance members. Eli will then pardon the resistance, disband the Death Squads and step down as

Grand Counsel,' Thomas said quickly. Sheeva couldn't help but notice that though they were victorious, Thomas looked defeated. 'I had hoped he would see the error of his ways and step down without coercion,' he said sadly.

'You can't save everyone, no matter how much you may want to Thomas,' Sheeva whispered, slipping her hand in his and squeezing it.

Chapter 31

Happy Families

'This was not the plan,' Helena screeched, tearing her hands through her hair. Her eyes were wild with anger. He had never seen her this way and it worried him. As much as Dragmir loved her he had to face the facts. She had been touched by a darkness ever since that day so many years ago. The day she had invoked ancient dark magic into her blood in order to kill Sophia. The blood of Hestia accomplished what was necessary but now he saw that it left scars on her soul. Helena had been utterly out of control when he found her. She had no idea the impact her powers had on those around her or the pain she caused. Helena had finally learned self-control with his help and it seemed as though they had a real chance of happiness. But then Sophia was born and everything changed. He could only imagine the guilt and sorrow she had carried since having to end their child's life and he dared not think what she might have done since she had been left alone. How had she lived with herself? Bereft of her love and responsible for the death of her child. His eyes filled with pity but she snorted as if sensing his thoughts.

'I know Helena but this may very well work out to our advantage. They are together now and that was the plan in the end. We just need to rethink a few things,' Dragmir cooed. He could not bring himself to deny her anything, not ever again. She had lost so much and suffered alone. He would give her anything and he had to admit a tiny part of him thought she was magnificent in her rage.

'What do you propose?'

'I propose we give them what they wanted all along,' Dragmir smiled coldly. 'Regina blames you for her father, her mother… pretty much everything. I say we use that.' Helena looked confused. 'They have Jay now, so there is every possibility they might just decide to try to return to the mortal world as soon as they can because of Regina's current state… but if you were to seek them out. How could she resist the urge to kill you?'

Helena grinned, her eyes lit with anticipation, 'I will let Sophia know.'

'No. We don't know how much self-control she has. If she kills them all before we can use them this has all been in vain,' Dragmir reasoned.

'She is much better than she was, I really think she can control herself,' Helena insisted.

'Maybe but are you willing to risk it?'

Helena sighed in defeat, she hated that he was right. As much as she would love to deny it Sophia had not improved as much as she had hoped. She feared she'd always been right about her; she could not change. That there was something innately wrong with her that was so bone-deep it could not be undone. Dragmir pulled Helena to him, his hands shook as he traced his finger along her cheekbone and tilted her chin. Helena gazed up at him, her eyes pools of deepest ebony.

'I still can't believe we're together again,' she breathed. It had been torture for them both being so close after all these years and yet not able to be together. It would be worth it in the end, she told herself again and again as she closed her eyes and revelled in his touch.

'Tell me again, why this is all necessary my love,' Dragmir said, his voice thick with emotion. He lifted her chin but she looked away.

'If we are to be free and together, this is the only way,' she breathed. She almost relented and melted right into him.

'We need to move fast, they are looking into the bracelet as we speak. We cannot allow them to succeed,' Dragmir brushed a stray hair from her face hooking it behind her ear. 'We have the element of surprise. They do not suspect who I am. You must attack whilst they believe me to be on their side.' He moved away reluctantly, his eyes drinking her in still not quite able to believe she was here with him. 'I will return to them and expect you just before nightfall.' His lips met Helena's for a brief kiss before he vanished into the already darkening evening.

D M Singh

Chapter 32

Reunited

Victory came at a price. It had been three weeks since they stormed the council chambers with a few newly trained resistance members and little hope of winning. Two of their number died following the attack, unable to recover from curses which had no cure.

The night Eli made his statement and stepped down, the safe house had erupted in cries of triumph with people toasting to the new order and most of all, celebrating that they could finally come out of hiding.

Thomas' eyes were blank as he watched the embers dancing in the fire of his study, choosing to closet himself away from the raucous merrymaking of the house. His finger tapped absently on the crystal highball glass which dangled from his long fingers. He should feel relief, happiness, pride... something. He felt nothing.

'Thought I might find you hiding in here,' Sheeva called from the doorway, before closing the door and settling next to him on the couch. She sat there for a minute in silence. Her eyes joining his watching the ballet within the flames.

'I feel it too,' she stated simply after a while, 'or rather I don't feel it.' Thomas looked at her, confusion in his eyes. 'This wasn't how it was supposed to be. Regina was supposed to be here, with us, Emile too and Evelyn...'

'What if we never see her again? What if Evelyn never wakes?' Thomas swallowed hard. 'While Eli was in power we had something to focus on, something to do, something good. Now...' He shoved his fingers through his hair sighing. A sound of pure despair and hopelessness which ripped at Sheeva's heart. 'I failed her. I thought Poppy would be able to keep her safe, that she could help her find her way back. I knew what it would mean if she entered The Darkness.'

'We all knew,' Sheeva asserted, 'and if you think for one minute any of us could have stopped her chasing that boy into The Darkness then I don't think you know her very well. I'm not talking about how powerful she is, I'm talking about her need to try and save everyone even if it costs her everything. She reminds me of someone I know.' She raised her brow, a hint of a smile on her lips.

'And what if Henry and Jane can't find the entrance to The Darkness?' Thomas continued.

'If anyone can find it, it's them. They want to get Regina back as much as we do. Their daughter is trapped there too,' Sheeva held Thomas' hands in hers, 'it can still work, she could be home anytime. We just have to have faith. We never thought we'd see the day Eli was removed from power and here we are. Anything is possible.'

'How do you always manage to see the best in everyone and everything?' Thomas said smiling into her eyes. 'And how do you always make me feel better, you're a miracle woman.' Thomas hesitated as if he was afraid of the moment, then his lips were on hers, slow and gentle. Sheeva's arms snaked up and into his hair.

She reluctantly broke the kiss, biting her lip thoughtfully, 'I think we should get back to the party. If we stay here much longer people will think I'm a nymph of ill-repute,' she giggled, 'you'll have to make an honest woman of me and stop all those wagging tongues.'

'Don't kid around Sheeva,' Thomas said suddenly serious, 'I've asked you so many times and you've shot me down every time. So don't say it unless you mean it.' His eyes searched hers.

'I'm completely serious. I thought I'd lost you for good,

I can't go through that again,' she shook her head banishing the memory. Thomas jumped from the couch and a second later was on his knee, a ring box in his hand. Sheeva's jaw dropped. 'When did you buy that?' She gasped.

'I've been carrying this in my pocket ever since you agreed to have dinner with me.' He flipped open the box to reveal a diamond ring, nestled inside. The band comprised entirely of diamonds and was shaped like the stalk of a flower which wove round a rose setting, made entirely of elven silver and diamonds.

'Sheeva, will you…?' Thomas started, but before he could finish Sheeva kissed him with such ferocity that for a moment, it all melted away and nothing else mattered. They broke apart breathing hard, Sheeva's eyes danced so happily he could not help but grin like a school boy. 'Should I take that as a yes?'

'Yes my reckless, thoughtful, crazy Thomas. You're mine now and forever. I hope you know what you're letting yourself in for,' she teased.

'I do,' Thomas said seriously as he grabbed her hand and slid the ring on.

'Come on, I want to tell your sister,' she squealed, delightedly and ran from the room, dragging him behind her.

D M Singh

Chapter 33

The Monster

'You're saying that Regina fed on you? But it wasn't Regina?' Aurora asked derisively. Her legs dangled from the armchair she was sat sideways on, in the library. She swung her legs, her long red skirt swirling as she did.

'I don't believe he was talking to you,' Imogen warned, her eyes flashing. Aurora snorted and rolled her eyes.

'Whatever, like I care anyway,' she leapt from her chair and disappeared out of the library.

'What do you mean it wasn't Regina?' Poppy asked, the red-headed nymph sat cross-legged on a desk filled with books and loose sheaves of paper.

'It was her but it wasn't her,' Jay groaned in frustration. He sounded crazy. 'It was like, when she loses control. You know … white eyes, looks scary as hell and eyes you up like you're an appetiser?'

'I'm all too familiar with that look,' Imogen grumbled.

'Well just when I thought I was done for, it… she talked to me. It sounded like Reggie but I knew it wasn't her. It was as if I was talking directly to her dark side… is this making any sense?' Jay rubbed the back of his neck, stopping in front of the chair Aurora had vacated and dropping into it.

'Not really but keep going it might start to,' Davina encouraged, her hand in Alexanders. The change in Davina since waking had been phenomenal, they all saw glimpses of Baby in her and they were beginning to see who she had been before The Darkness had filled her so completely.

Jay recounted their conversation, how she had reasoned

with him and even shown concern over taking too much blood and killing him. The others looked stunned. Being only the second of her kind in existence they had no way to know what this meant. Or why this version of Regina felt she needed Jay's blood.

Since her night time visit, Regina had kept to her room and refused to let Jay in. Instead she remained silent on the other side of the door, ignoring Jay's pleas for her to let him in.

'So does Regina… our Regina know what the other Regina did and why?' Poppy wondered. Her question was met with shaking heads and shrugs around the room.

'Is this a private party?' A familiar yet unfamiliar voice demanded from the doorway. Regina perched herself on the arm of the chair Jay was occupying. White blank eyes blazed out at them. Poppy swallowed hard, Davina grasped Alexander's hand tightly, her eyes filled with fear.

'I'm not here to hurt you. You have questions for me I hear?' She raised her brow in question. Imogen just stared open mouthed, struck dumb. This was what they had always feared, that Regina would become this thing.

'Is she ok?' Jay asked, longing in his voice.

'She's fine. It's like she's sleeping. At least that's what it feels like when I'm dormant,' Regina's monster shrugged.

'Why did you need Jay's blood and why do you want to help us?' Imogen finally found her voice.

'Well it's not really you I'm helping, it's me. Like I explained to lover-boy last night, we are one and the same and this…' She rolled the sleeve of her shirt up to her elbow to reveal the painful looking barbs, 'will kills us both if it is permitted to continue spreading. His blood calls to her but she resists because she fears she might kill him. There is a reason your blood calls to her elf.'

'You think my blood could reverse the process?' Jay

said incredulously.

'I don't think… I know.' She rolled the sleeve higher to her shoulder, the barbs had disappeared. Jay laughed and grabbed her arm, skimming his hands over the clear, healed skin. Regina's monster growled a warning, yanking her arm free.

'Don't touch me!' She spat furiously, 'I only have so much control elf,' her biting tone snapped Jay back to reality.

'Could it work?' Poppy asked Alexander excitedly, her large eyes brightening at the prospect that she might get her friend back.

'It already seems to be working,' he declared, 'I have no idea why, but yes it would seem it could save her.' Davina smiled up at him and he planted a kiss on her forehead.

'You need more,' Jay said, understanding now why she had revealed herself to all of them. She nodded.

'I don't have long. Once she is back in control she will stop you. She is more concerned with harming you than saving herself.'

'Okay,' Jay said determined.

'Hey where did Dragmir go?' Imogen asked suddenly, 'I've not seen him for hours.'

'He said he had a friend he wanted to try and find while we're here,' Alexander said.

'Did he say who?' Imogen asked, something wasn't right with him but so far she just couldn't prove it.

'His maker I think?' Davina said. 'Why?'

'He's been gone a lot lately don't you think?' Imogen mused.

'Perhaps he has had bother locating his friend. It's not like you can look them up on Facebook in this place,' Poppy shrugged. Imogen nodded but was not appeased.

'Shall we?' Jay said opening the door for the other Regina, the one he had thought a monster, now he wasn't sure what to make of her. She nodded and followed him to the study next door.

Chapter 34

Own Worst Enemy

Gloomy shadows scattered and moaned across the deserted walls of the castle. Something was coming. Something powerful, something dangerous. The demons shrieked and fled.

On the south side of the castle evil stirred, waiting for a way in, for a way to destroy Regina once and for all. A door opened in the earth and a hooded figure dressed in black quickly descended the steps into the murky depths of the castle's dungeons.

★ ★ ★ ★ ★ ★ ★ ★ ★

'NO!' Regina screamed. She quickly sprang back from Jay as he slumped back in the chair, pale and unmoving. Her chin dripped with his sweet tasting blood and her stomach turned as she realised she wanted more. Regina grabbed him and shook him, his head lolled from side to side. She screamed as her heart splintered into a million pieces. She'd killed him. What had she done? She didn't even remember attacking him. She pulled the door open frantically looking for help.

'Dad, Poppy, Dragmir, Davina, Alexander…' She called to the cavernous, echoing hallways. Her voice filled with panic. She could NOT lose him again. Where was everybody? Then a thought occurred to her, what if she gave him her blood? She didn't know if it would work or what it might do to him if it did but she just could not lose another person she loved.

Regina plunged her fangs into her wrist and dripped her blood onto his lips. There was still no movement. She grasped his face and pressed his lips to her wrist, silently screaming for him to drink. For four long seconds nothing, then he began to drink gently at first, and then as if he were in the desert and her blood was the coolest water in an oasis. His eyes drifted open and met hers, full of so much longing and intensity that Regina blushed.

'I thought I'd lost you,' she stammered, tears sticking in her throat as she pulled him close.

'You'll never lose me. I'm like superglue,' he winked before swooping in for a kiss. Her blood was still in his mouth spilled into her lips and she gasped as he deepened the kiss, kissing her as if scared she might change her mind. When she finally pulled away she was breathless and her eyes shone with happiness.

'What happened? I don't even remember waking up this morning. One minute I was asleep, the next I was here... draining you,' a little sob escaped her. Was she really losing her mind?

'I'll explain everything but first let me show you something,' he pulled her to her feet dancing her across the room to a mirror. Standing behind her he gently tugged her sleeve up.

Regina gasped, 'it's gone, but how?' She ran her hands where the barbs had been. It was completely clear.

'How do you feel?' Jay asked anxiously.

'Like myself again,' she breathed a sigh of relief, she had been a prisoner inside this place, in her body, in her mind. It felt good to be free.

'What about you? I gave you my blood. How do you feel?' She asked tentatively.

'I don't know, I don't feel any different. So I guess I'm fine.' He shrugged and Regina scowled wondering if he really was or if in her haste to save him she may have done unknown damage. Jay spun her around to face him so quickly her breath caught in her throat. She suddenly felt like a teenager and not an immensely powerful supernatural being. For that second she was just Reggie and she sighed as she held onto the boy she loved.

'What was that?' Jay whispered forcing himself to break contact with Regina. A thud echoed through the castle. She stiffened and twisted the bracelet around her wrist nervously. She had tried removing it but it wouldn't budge. At least it wasn't trying to bury itself into her like a giant worm for the moment.

'The others,' Regina panicked. She quickly ran to the door, hoping the others were okay. Jay called her as she ran but she didn't stop until she reached the library where they all generally congregated. The door opened as she approached as if expecting her.

The smell of blood hit her as soon as she entered the room and she was instantly transported back to her bedroom at home. Her mother pleading for her to run and her father dead on the floor. Helena was poised to slide that blade across her mother's throat once more. What was going on? She closed her eyes and shook her head. Still Helena stood there. She couldn't watch this again, it was too much. Her father's still body brought tears to her eyes as she flew across the room. She gripped Helena by the throat pinning her to the wall. Helena's feet flailed wildly as she tried to break free. Jay's footsteps echoed down the corridor and he called to Regina but before he could reach her the door slammed refusing him entry. He hammered on the door, screaming for Regina to open up.

'What is this?' Regina asked, her eyes white with fury.

'This is your chance to save them,' Helena choked out. Regina loosened her grip, just enough for her to talk. 'What would you say if I told you that you could have them back?'

'What's the catch? And why on earth would I believe you?' Regina screamed, it took every ounce of self-control not to rip her heart out.

'Why would I risk coming? I'm nothing if not practical Regina. I want to return to the mortal world. You are the key. If you do this, your parents get to live and I get what I want. It's win-win.'

'I SAID what's the catch?' Regina ground out.

'Fine. You've got me there is catch. For it to work you have to kill an innocent, muddy your hands with their blood,' Helena grinned.

'I already have my father, he's here and my mother… well we'll figure that out when I get back,' Regina returned. She dropped Helena, her eyes still trained on her.

'Oh no! Didn't daddy dearest tell you?' She pouted. 'He can't return any other way. I made sure of that with a little hex I cooked up, as for your mother, well she'll be trapped in-between forever. You know you really should have let her die. At least they would have been together. Children, so selfish.' Regina's face paled. If this was the only way, she couldn't bring herself to do it. It was wrong, she had fought so hard not to become a monster, she wasn't about to give in. She shook her head, sickened that she would once again be without her parents. She had to act now before she gave in to it. 'Think about it Regina, are you really willing to leave your little friends stranded here just because you haven't got the bottle to off some little nothing demon?'

'We'll find another way,' Regina said more confidently than she felt. The door opened behind her and Jay was at her side.

'Do it Reggie,' Jay said quietly. Regina looked confused.

'Take us home, take us all home,' Poppy, Alexander, Davina, Imogen, Emile, Evelyn and Aurora all entered the room. Much to Regina's surprise, they did not attack. Instead they stared blankly ahead.

'What did you do to them?' Regina demanded.

'Oh stop being so dramatic child, they'll be fine,' Helena snapped impatiently. The door slammed once more and from the other side she could hear Jay telling her to let him in.

'If Jay's out there who is he?' Regina spun back and was confronted with Dragmir.

'I see you're acquainted with my darling wife,' Dragmir grinned, taking Helena's hand and kissing it.

Her head spun, 'how could you?'

'Quite easily actually. Do you know how long I have been alone in here?' He bellowed. For the first time since she had met Dragmir she did not see her father in his ways. His face was twisted in a cruel smile. He was enjoying it. Was this what this place did to people? She couldn't stand this one second longer, she had to stop Helena before she hurt anyone else. Even if it meant she was stuck here forever. Helena seemed to sense the attack and shoved Dragmir out of the way. It was over in a moment. Honestly she had expected more of a fight but Helena just stopped fighting. Regina was at her throat before Dragmir could stop her. She ripped till the blood soaked her chest and dripped down to the floor. She spun around ready to face Dragmir and instead she found Helena and Dragmir. Her head whipped back to where she had thrown Helena's gasping, dying body. There lying in a growing lake of blood was Jay. He was desperately trying to hold his throat together as he shuddered, his eyes wide and full of disbelief. The room, a library once more held only Regina's cries and Jay's silent screams as he tried to hold on to his last breaths.

D M Singh

Chapter 35

Back home

'No, no, no, no!' Regina chanted over and over, puncturing her wrist once more and dripping the crimson liquid into Jay's mouth. Pleading over and over with him. She felt a slicing on her other wrist and turned to see Helena using a hexed blade to remove the bracelet.

'I'll take care of this don't worry. I really should thank you Regina. Thanks to you I have my husband, my daughter, a brand new shiny army of the undead and this little lovely,' She dangled the bracelet, 'and no-one to stop me.' Dragmir and Helena fled the room. Outside, the sound of spells ricocheting off the walls filled Regina with dread. The door burst open once more and Poppy and Imogen ran toward a now blood soaked Regina. Jay twitched and then stopped moving. Regina screamed, a horrible feral sound that chased Helena and Dragmir down the hall.

'What happened? Who did this?' Poppy asked the now numb Regina.

'Helena of course,' Imogen said, 'she and Dragmir took off like bats out of hell. I knew there was something dodgy about him. I knew I'd heard his name before. Reggie I'm so sorry, this is my fault.'

Regina shook her head, 'not Helena.' She squeaked out. 'I did it.' She collapsed in heaps of shuddering sobs. 'I thought he was her. I mean… I was in my bedroom and you were there and then Jay was there but then he was Dragmir and then I killed Helena, only Helena wasn't Helena she was Jay. I tried to give him my blood but it's not working… why isn't it working?' She rocked back

233

and forth in his blood. 'Did I kill him Immy? Did I? I can't have. He can't be gone.' She stared down at her hands dripping with his blood. 'I am a monster,' she said quietly. Poppy and Imogen exchanged a look of disbelief.

'She said this would open the way to the mortal world,' Regina whispered, 'we need to stop her but I can't leave him.'

'I'll find out what's happening,' Imogen volunteered, 'you stay with Jay.'

'I'll come with you,' Poppy called, chasing her out of the door. They couldn't get away fast enough and Regina couldn't blame them.

She sat there in his cooling lifeblood as it pooled around her. Stroking his jet black hair, her fingers lingering on his blue streak. As she did, she could have sworn she saw a finger twitch. Then suddenly his chest arched up before thudding back down. His eyes flew open, completely black and fixed on her.

'You killed me,' he accused. Regina was so relieved he was moving and breathing that she momentarily lost her tongue. 'To think I thought that I loved you,' he growled baring his teeth. It seemed he had been changed by her blood after all. It was like a knife to the heart to hear the spite in his usual cheerful voice but at least he was alive.

'We found them,' Imogen barrelled back through the door, 'we need to go now.' Regina nodded and got to her feet.

'Jay? How are you alive right now?' Imogen said amazed.

'Her blood's good for something it seems.' He hugged Imogen and Regina bristled at how long he lingered. She had a feeling he did it on purpose.

'Let's go,' Regina growled. 'Where're the others?'

'Poppy went to find them. They'll meet us there,' Imogen said, wrenching away from Jay.

In the middle of the dusty, darkened land at the north side of the castle, a rip had appeared, growing in size. At the very front stood Sophia, her hands in the air, barking orders like a warrior queen of old to the demon army she now commanded. From the castle's drawbridge Regina saw Dragmir and Helena making their way to the back of the rows and rows of soldiers.

'What have I done?' Regina whispered, her eyes filling with tears.

'Looks like you've handed Helena the mortal world. Oh and you killed me twice today,' Jay seethed as he stalked past after Helena and Dragmir. Imogen looked at Regina for answers but she just shook her head, she didn't have the energy to explain something she didn't understand herself. In the distance Regina could see Poppy, Emile, Alexander, Davina and Aurora searching through the crowds for them, presumably.

Swallowing the guilt and pain down, Regina trekked after Jay with Imogen trailing behind. Hordes of undead demons rushed the entrance to the mortal world. They were too late, the invasion had begun. She had to do something. This was her doing. She had been so hell-bent on revenge that she hadn't seen it was a trick.

Leaping into the air she skimmed above the assembled army, who gawked up at the strange sight. The ground beneath her cracked as she landed and placed herself firmly between the rest of the dead and the entryway.

'So this is the other one,' a curious voice pondered. Regina found herself face to face with Sophia. 'I thought you'd be taller,' she shrugged. 'So... sister, how do you like my army?' She had a manic look in her eyes that scared Regina, this was not Sophia's monster, this was her and she was excited.

'What do you plan to do once you've crossed over?' Regina asked cautiously.

'Oh the usual, revenge, world domination, that kind of

thing.' She inspected her nails nonchalantly as if she was already bored of this interaction.

'Well that's not going to happen,' Jay stated confidently, as he landed beside Regina. In the flickering of the light Regina blanched at the blackness of his eyes. And she wondered if Helena's tricks had another purpose. His sudden personality transplant scared her. He was her only constant, she needed him and dreaded to think what she might become without him. He gave her a tiny lop-sided grin and her heart fluttered with hope.

'Wow! Who's the eye candy?' Sophia licked her lips and Regina growled in response. 'Don't fret sister dear, I don't want your sloppy seconds. Shame though.' Her eyes lingered on Jay again, who scowled back at her.

Jay fired a spell at Sophia but she laughed as it hit her. She grabbed him by the throat, her fangs bared ready to tear at his flesh. Regina flinched, as Jay's own fangs descended surprising them all. Sophia grinned maliciously and pulled him into her, crashing her lips to his for a moment before he pulled away, a look of disgust on his face. 'Interesting,' she mused, as if she was conducting a scientific study.

'Get your hands off my boyfriend,' Regina screeched. All pretence of playing it cool was obliterated at the sight of Sophia lip-locked with Jay. Jay flashed her a look of longing, before his eyes flashed back to black and it was replaced with hate. Ignoring the pain of her heart tearing, Regina grabbed Sophia and threw her back towards the hoards who had not yet entered the tear. Sophia emitted a banshee-like chilling cry that sent shivers down Regina's spine.

'I'll end you,' Sophia seethed. She flung demons left and right, they crumpled and broke as she made her way towards them once more. Jay's eyes flashed towards Regina and for a second he looked worried and flew through the air landing in Sophia's path. He had always been powerful but whatever Regina's blood had done to him had made him even more so.

'I don't think so,' Jay warned. His tone so ice-cold that Regina barely recognised him. 'You're not touching her and you're most definitely not returning to the mortal world.'

'Brave words little elf. It's a shame I'll have to kill you. You're not a bad kisser.'

'ENOUGH!' Helena's voice rang out. She and Dragmir along with a smug looking Aurora had joined the throng of demons filtering around Jay and Sophia. 'We don't have time to play with your little friends daughter dear, we have an apocalypse to usher in.' She touched her finger to the bracelet she had torn from Regina's wrist and muttered a spell.

'Stop her!' Regina cried. Too late; a cloud of purple mist enveloped them and when it lifted they were gone: Dragmir, Helena, Aurora, Sophia and the entire undead army.

'Where did they go?' Jay asked, his eyes darting around.

'There,' Regina said numbly. Her eyes were glued to the tear where a purple mist had appeared and sparked as it disappeared through.

'We have to go,' Poppy insisted as she caught up, closely followed by the others. Her eyes were filled with panic. She fled into the tear, followed by Imogen. Jay cast Regina a look which set her teeth on edge, he was not her Jay right now and her heart broke.

'Time to go love,' Emile said softly as Davina and Alexander jumped into the tear. Regina nodded silently. She lifted her head and met her father's gaze, the tears there told her that this was one thing Helena had not lied about. Her father would not be joining her in the mortal world.

'I can't dad,' she choked, 'I can't go on. I just try so

hard to save everyone, to help everyone, to do the right thing but I only make it worse.'

'That's not true,' Emile said gently brushing her tears away.

'Let's look at the evidence shall we? As soon as I changed into this thing, I turned my back on you and mum, which led to your death and mum becoming Casper the friendly ghost. Mrs Kettleworth was killed, Poppy was killed, the resistance was raided and hundreds were murdered. Jay was pulled into The Darkness, I killed him twice today and now hell has literally been unleashed on Earth,' she rattled off. 'Did I miss anything?' She said with a hint of bitterness.

'None of that was your fault Reggie. You are not to blame for the evil that has found its way to your doorstep. You are this world's greatest chance of survival. It's not fair and I wish I could take your place but I can't. Watching you fight to stay who you are, and never giving up on your friends has made me prouder than you'll ever know.' He pulled her close, clinging to her for a second before releasing her to look down into her watery eyes. 'Now, I do believe you have a world to save and a boy to win back,' He smiled in approval and Regina blushed.

'What about you?' She bit her lip, eager to follow Jay and find a way to bring the old him back.

'I'll be fine. Now that you have righted this place, it should improve here. I think I can be a real help. I always did enjoy a bit of DIY,' he grinned, 'it's a big project but it'll keep me busy till I see my girls again.' Regina dove back into his arms, tears slicing down her face.

'I'll see you soon Reggie,' he whispered. She nodded, unable to speak and walked away before she could change her mind. The winds screamed now, an inhumanly evil sound that chilled Regina through. And as the abyss of dark and despair enveloped her, all she could think was, Helena was right, then her eyes closed in surrender and with no more fight left in her, she felt the world tear open and she fell.

D M Singh

Chapter 36

Unleashed

A snap of a branch alerted Jane. She leaned back into the shadows, her eye's searching, hoping it would be him. Muffled footsteps were followed by his familiar scent of sandalwood. Jane emerged from the shadows, a ghost of a smile upon her face.

It had been mere weeks since Imogen had entered The Darkness. Jane and Henry had remained Helena's captives and by the time Sheeva had seen to their release, Imogen had already followed her friend. Jane could still recall the moment Thomas had broken the news. She'd felt every ounce of strength abandon her, a mist of despair all but threatening to consume her forever. She could not imagine life without her daughter. Henry had stood, jaw clenched, knuckles white, staring into nothing. Jane couldn't really blame Imogen for wanting to help Regina, after all, they had led her like a lamb to the slaughter - albeit unknowingly. Sure she had known Helena was not the warm fuzzy type but she had never imagined her real purpose in 'rescuing' Regina. She shuddered thinking at what might have been, had she not acted and told her to flee.

'Any word?' Jane asked hopefully as Henry approached.

'No,' he drew her to him, relishing her closeness. They had been alone these past weeks, and though they'd much to sadden them, they had become closer than ever.

'I'm sure if they discover anything they would let us know,' Jane said decisively.

Thomas had asked the two vampires to take on an essential mission. So they had journeyed to Bouvet Island, a desolate place consisting of ice cliffs and little else. This was where the door between this world and The Darkness would appear should someone manage to break through. Thomas managed to decipher as much from some of the files they had taken from the elf archives. And While Jane and Henry were unable to open the door from this side, it could be opened on the other. The thought filled Jane with a sprinkle of hope and that was what carried her through.

Henry was changed. Helena's betrayal had cut him deeper than it had the others. He had known her for as long as he could remember and though he always had a sensible amount of fear for her as his elder, he had never imagined she could be so cruel. He leapt at the chance to help and though he too was eager to see Imogen, he was also eager to see Helena again. Henry was never violent, as ridiculous as that sounded for someone who fed on the blood of others. He drank from blood reserves and if he ever had to feed on a human, he made sure it was painless and they had no memory of his assault. So it was disturbing for Jane to see the changes in him. Even his appearance seemed altered, his face dressed in a seemingly permanent five o' clock shadow and darkness now haunted his once bright eyes.

Gathering the supplies they needed had been

difficult. Many of the items on the list Thomas had supplied them with were rare and hard to procure. Jane had managed to get most of them from a nearby troll commune. She had always been charming as a human but as a vampire most found it impossible to refuse her anything. Henry had left the island to secure the last few herbs from the mainland, while she prepared.

'It wasn't hard to find,' Henry said dumping a pouch onto a lump of ice next to the other ingredients. 'The witch I bought it from was very suspicious. Thank goodness Martha thought to give us the *'innocence'* potion. A quick whiff of that and she handed it over, no questions asked.'

'We're ready,' Jane said, hope creeping into her voice. Together they read the instructions, chopped, sliced, ground and mixed, careful to follow each direction exactly. They could not afford to get this wrong. If this was done correctly, the spell would act as a worm-hole of sorts, which would activate once they opened the doorway from the other side.

'Mindkét birodalmakban,' Jane whispered over and over as she daubed the paste on a wall of solid ice. Henry opened a phial he had kept on a cord around his neck and threw the contents at the centre of the doorway they created. Jane murmured the incantation one more time and the paste sprouted flames before quickly dying.

'Do you think it worked?'

'I guess we'll find out soon enough,' Henry shrugged, before propping himself against the wall, a sigh of exhaustion escaping his lips. But Jane remained vigilant, unable to tear her eyes from the ice-wall, willing them to appear. She was sure the reappearance of Imogen would have Henry back to his old self in no time. They had endured much in Helena's cells. The unending pain she could cope with but it was the promise of what would become of Imogen that terrified Jane. She had slept little since they'd been freed and when she did, flashes of that place and the unspeakable things Aurora did to them haunted her dreams. Being awake gave her even less solace. The guilt she carried for her part in what had happened to Regina weighed on her heavily. Jane could not help but think that if Regina and the others did not return that her eternity would be forever filled with nightmares and guilt.

In the corner of the cave Evelyn moaned quietly to herself. A tiny sound really, a shift in her breathing pattern, but enough for both vampires to notice.

'Is she?' Jane wondered aloud.

'Waking up?' Henry said at the same time. 'What does this mean?'

Thomas had asked them to take Evelyn with them when they left. He had insisted that if he failed in his plan and Regina did not return, he wanted Evelyn safe.

'There,' Jane cried pointing, a look of excitement and trepidation washing across her face. 'Her hand moved. See!' Sure enough, Evelyn's hand twitched, then made a fist. Her eyelids fluttered opened and Evelyn's big green eyes opened fully settling on the two vampires. She opened her mouth but nothing came. She flapped her hands urgently, trying to get up with no success.

'Her wand,' Henry said quickly, rushing to find

Jane's bag and digging out the wand. Taking the wand from henry, Evelyn swept it down her body from head to toe, then stretched and stood.

'I don't have long, this spell will only strengthen me a short time,' her voice was panicked. She cast her eyes towards the newly created doorway and sighed with relief, 'good. They have not returned yet.' Jane and Henry looked confused. What was happening? Surely Evelyn wanted Regina back. 'They are coming, all of them. You have to seal the doorway. NOW!' She gasped as though this was her last bit of strength.

'You don't understand Evelyn, you've been under a spell for a long time...' Henry said piteously.

'I understand just fine Henry. I have heard and seen everything, I was trapped in The Darkness. I don't know how but somehow I'm free but before I awoke I saw what was coming. You cannot...' Evelyn did not finish. Gusts of wind swept through the cave and ice cracked below their feet. Outside the cave, thunder rumbled in the dark and a flash of light sliced through the entrance, almost close enough to touch.

'What's happening Henry?' Jane screamed into the chaotic din. The ground shook once more and the two vampires took flight, hovering a few feet from the ground as it continued to shake and crumble beneath them. Henry swept a now spent Evelyn into his arms.

The wind dropped suddenly and for a second all was silent, Jane shot a quizzical look at her husband, who looked just as lost as she.

'They are coming,' Evelyn whispered in the quiet.

Her face pale and eyes small with fear.

The doorway burned and Jane watched it hopefully, searching the depths for a sign of Imogen but Henry moved further away beckoning her to follow.

'Jane, come away,' he called but it was too late. The explosion threw Henry across the cave, he struggled to prop himself. Evelyn was right to be afraid. He was pretty sure he was looking at hell on Earth. Scores of demons, dragon and Lost Souls walked through the doorway, their red eyes hungry and fixed on him.

Coming 2017

Regina: Demons from the Ashes

By D M Singh

The world is at war. The demons of the immortal realms have been unleashed upon the mortal realm. Can Regina and the resistance find a way to save us, or is this the end?

D M Singh

Coming 2016

Dead
Normal?
By D M Singh

Sneak-peek
(enjoy)
-Prologue-

People say it's not what you have, but what you've

done with your life that matters in the end. I'd have to disagree. Mostly because when I died, I had a lot of stuff but hadn't done much of anything with my life, but then again I did die way before my time. Before I'd even had chance to experience a lot of firsts in my life.

So what can be said for my life? The obituary in the local paper didn't quite capture the truth behind my death.

> Lily Elizabeth Reynolds. Died tragically 23rd June 2011 aged 23. Leaves behind a loving Father Henry, Devoted Mother Enid and younger sister Jennifer. Funeral will be held at All Saints Church Monday 4th July 2011 at 10am, internment to follow at Rodsforth Cemetery all flowers to be sent to D&M Funeral Home, Ridgley Avenue, Greendale.

The facts of this are stricly correct. Yes I was 23 and yes I died but perhaps a truer interpretation would be - Lily Renolds 23, died at a music festival when a van backed into the portaloo she was pooping in, causing it to roll down the bank and into oncoming traffic, where she was promptly squashed. It's not pretty, not glamorous but it's what happened. Then again, perhaps I should be glad they had printed a toned down version. It sure would have got a lot of laughs though.

Chapter One

- Hello Death -

When you hear people talking about near-death experinces and how they look down on their bodies whilst floating like some eatheral being, they make it sound like such a spiritual experience. This was not the case for me. Looking down on my bloody mangled corpse, with limbs twisted in awkward positions and seeing my skull crushed and covered in excrement, was not a spiritual experience. I was lucky I guess that I hit my head on the way down the bank, and was gone before I was squashed by the delivery truck. It should have been a time of reflection or disbelief but all I could think was, damn! No open casket. That led to the giggles, which quickly turned to panic when I realised that this wasn't near-death. This was death.

I shouted at the ambulance crew as they arrived on the scene. Waved my hands in front of their faces. Nothing. No-one could see or hear me. I even tried throwing the toilet seat at the policeman who was stood turning traffic away from the accident, but I couldn't even pick it up.

So I sat and watched and waited as they cleared me away. I remember thinking they'd have better luck with a cartoon-style giant spatula to scrape me off the road. They managed it in the end. Then they were gone, and so was I. Nothing left at the scene except some police tape and a large crimson pool of blood.

What now? I was stood on a dual-carriageway with no clue what would happen next. I glanced at the floor relieved that no firey pits had opened up to swallow me but then again no angels appeared to sweep me away to a better place.

That's when I met Derek but you might know him better as death. At first I thought he was a lookey-loo, come to see the dead poop girl just a little too late. To my surprise however, he looked right at me.

'Hey,' he drawled. His voice was gravelly and he sounded kind of stoned.

'You can see me?' I squeaked.

'Sure,' he said, looking me up and down in a way that made my skin crawl. Urgh are there still creeps after death? Gross!

'So what are you? Like a ghost whisperer or something?' I asked, when he volunteered nothing more.

'No I'm death,' he said glibly, sitting cross legged on the floor and leaning back his on his hands, eyes cast skyward.

'You're death?' I asked sardonically. This was not what I had expected. Wasn't death supposed wear a cloak and carry a sythe? I took in his faded black t-shirt, shaggy blonde hair that looked allergic to shampoo, ripped jeans and battered trainers.

'Yeah, but you can call me Derek,' he said simply, eyes still skyward. That was too much, I erupted into hysterics. This was all too much, death by toilet and now I was chatting to death, who just happened to be called Derek. My after-life so far was not living up to the hype. 'That's a new one,' Derek quipped, as he stood back up to inspect me. His eyes were so dark brown they were almost black, they bored right through me in a profoundly unsettling way. I shuddered. 'That's more like it,' he grinned. 'Most people in your position are in denial and trying to strike a bargain with me by now.' He cocked his head, brow arched, waiting expectantly for me to beg for mercy. I didn't.

'I'm not most people,' I bristled. 'So what happens now?' I asked looking around for clue of where I was supposed to be moving onto. Surely the appearance of Death meant that there had to be a heaven?

'Let's see shall we?' Derek clicked his fingers and a heat seared through my whole body followed by a blindling light. The next moment we were in a grotty looking derelict office with Derek perched on a chair behind a cluttered old desk, shuffling through some files.

I sat impatiently contemplating what had tranpisred and for the first time worried for my soul, had I blown it? I never really commited to a religion when I was alive, but I'd always hoped that there was something better to look forward to than being thrown in a hole in the ground waiting for insects to join the all you can eat buffet.

Cremation, had always given me the creeps, I remember when I was about 5 years old sitting next to my mother at my Grandfathers funeral, while she prattled on about how cremetion worked. Needless to say I was horrifed by the graphic picture she painted in my head. Mum was many things but tactful was not amongst them. I woke up screaming every night for a week convinced someone would think I was dead and set my bed alight. So unlike most people of 23 I had already made my funeral plans clear, there would be no cremetion.

'Aha!' Derek cried slapping a file down in front of him and grinning widely, a thick swirl of dust took flight from the bowning pages, shocking me from my morbid reverie. 'I knew I saw you lying around here somewhere yesterday,' he ran his finger along the lines his mouth moving soundlessly as he searched.

'Lily, age 23, no significant relationships or children, still at university after repeating your final year and still living at home. Does that sound right?' I nodded. It was an accurate but very depressing summary of my very short life. As I began feeling sorry for myself I wondered if ghosts could suffer from depression before something Derek had said snapped me out of it. 'Hang on, you said you saw my file hanging about yesterday?' My mind was whirring, what did this mean? Was I destined to die on the pooper. Wow what a destiny.

'Erm…actually it's been floating around for a while, but I only processed your paperwork yesterday.' He looked sheepish and plopped back into a ratty chair with stuffing poking out from the seat another cloud of dust erupted in protest as he sat.

'Would you mind translating for those of us in the room who don't speak death?' I shot sarcastically.

'Sure,' he smirked. 'Basically when your times up, it's up but it's up to me to do the paperwork. Your file came a month ago, but I've only just gotten around to it. So here you are.' He gestured to the room at large, as if being here were a prize on the world's worst game show.

'So I should have died a month ago?' My voice shrilled, I always hated it when it got that way. I always imagined whales tipping over and dogs running in circles everytime it did.

'Technically you should have died...' he glanced down at the file. ' four weeks ago in a car crash, death on impact.' he snapped the file shut, as I leaned over to try and catch a glimpse.

'So instead of dying in a tragic accident and being wept over by friends and family, I'm now the poop girl?' I could hear the anger in my voice and knew it was ridiculous after all, dead is dead.

'Sorry for giving you the extra time, but if I recall I did hear you say that if you could just see Rage Against The Machine once before you die you'd be happy.'

'What? I meant I really, really wanted to see them, not that I wanted to roll down a hill into traffic. with poo in my hair and then. How do you know anyway? That was just chit chat to some stoner in the … that was you?' Before I could stop myself I had launched myself across the desk in a attempt to slap that smug grin off his face, but he disapeared and my face collided with the still spinning chair he had vacated.

'You think you're the first to take a swing at me?' He laughed from behind me, making me jump. I closed my eyes and took a deep breath, was I even breathing? Or did the process just make me feel alive, I wasn't sure of anything anymore. I opened my eyes forcing calm into my voice.

'What happens next Derek?' I ground out the words carefully, my fists balled at my side. Derek nodded, assured I was not going to go psycho on him, at least for the moment and flitted back to his dust coated chair.

'According to this you're not ready to move on, so it looks like your stuck here a while longer,' he snapped the file shut, as I edged forwards to try and scan the contents.

'Here?' I gestured to the room, unimpressed.

'Not here, but your not ready to leave the mortal world just yet. According to my paperwork, you have four essential experiences left before you can move on.' He leaned back in his chair. It sqeauked and made a terrible cracking noise as if it might give under the strain. Derek ran his long fingers through his hair and watched me expectantly, his brow furrowed and those impossibly black eyes searched my face, making me feel very small and insignificant. I paced back in forth, just to avoid that unerving stare.

'So, I'm not moving on yet but I will?'

'Correct.'

'As soon as I've had those ... four experiences, I will?' This was making my head hurt, or perhaps I imagined it did, seeing as technically my head was on its way to a mortuary somewhere to be identified. I drifted for a moment, wondering how long it would be before they called my parents. Everything suddenly became very real in that moment. My parents and my little sister Jennifer, how would they take it? Would dad start drinking again? Would mum even cry? I'd never known her to shed a tear, even when her mother died. Would they call Jennifer out of her class. I suddenly felt incredibly guilty. I knew it was ridiculous, after all I hadn't died on purpose but imagining them having to cope with this, made me feel like the worst daughter ever.

'When you say I'll move on, what exactly does that mean?' I glanced heavenward suerruptiously, as I perched on the arm of an armchair leaking it's innards.

'Now that would be telling.' Derek quipped, leaning forward across his desk, his cold black eyes suddenly glinting with mischief. Was death really messing with me?

'You mean you don't know?' I shot back leaning back, crossing my arms a knowing look on my face.

'What's the matter? Not high up enough in the company to know the next step?' My knowing look quickly faded as his eyes flashed with anger at my remark, and I immediatley regretted my words. Me and my smart mouth, why did I never think before I spoke? I was talking to death for goodness sake and I still couldn't watch my mouth.

Death's eyes were a-flame and his lips curled upwards, a shudder ran through me involuntarily. I blanched but held my head high, as usual my mouth had run ahead of sense and reason.

'Follow me,' he ground the words out as he strode to the door and opened it, indicating for me to exit his office. I took a deep breath and walked through.

About the Author

Dawn's debut novel Regina: The Monster Inside was released in 2014 and was the first of a trilogy. The final book in the trilogy is planned for release in 2017. She is also currently on a stand-alone novel called Dead Normal, due for release this year.

Dawn is heavily influenced by YA novels, Sci-fi and fantasy, being a huge fan of the genres and is a self-confessed nerd.

She currently resides with her husband, two daughters, son and cat Mario in West Yorkshire. Dawn is currently the director of The UK Indie Literature Festival, which she will be appearing at this July.

For more information on this and other projects by D M Singh go to

www.dmsinghwriting.wix.com/author

16965369R00144

Printed in Great Britain
by Amazon